LAST ONE TO LEAVE

For Josephine

4 CONTESTANTS REMAINING

ExtractedAudio_LiveStream_Filtered.wav

Lisa: There's so much blood.

May: Oh my God.

Ryan: Maybe it's . . . I mean . . . Is it for real this time?

Lisa: Of course it's real.

May: I think I can smell blood.

Lisa: When did you . . .?

Ryan: I just woke up.

Lisa: Someone check.

Michelle: You'd like that, wouldn't you? I'm not moving.

May: It could be another trick.

Lisa: There's a fucking dead body in the middle of the room. Someone do something!

Michelle: I'm not falling for it.

May: Actually, yeah. Why wasn't there a horn?

Lisa: Anybody? Hello? Can you hear us or are you just sitting there and watching, you sick bastards? Anybody? Help! *Help*!

7 CONTESTANTS
REMAINING

ONE

One week prior

'Daaaaaad,' Lydia's groan was long and drawn out, pulling the word like chewing gum from her teeth. 'Don't be so *lame.*'

As an insult, it didn't really hold up to the scornful tirades Ryan was used to at work, which usually had as many hyphenated swear words as the refused-service drunks could string together, but his daughter's simplicity was more cutting. Because she could only put it simply, and simple was far closer to the truth. When *had* he become so lame?

'I'm not *lame,*' Ryan said, scanning the yellow discount tickets for a pre-made Mexican kit that was almost the same as the ones Lydia actually liked. She was nearby, having invented a game with the trolley: gently pushing it to see how far it would roll down the aisle before chasing after it. 'Who's going to look after you?'

She puffed out her chest. 'I can look after myself.'

'You can't even eat without spilling food down your front.' Ryan pointed to her shirt and, when she looked down to see nothing there, flicked his finger up into her nose.

She dissolved into giggles, but then folded her arms and pouted in mock betrayal. 'Don't change the topic.'

'Honey.' He ruffled her hair, settled on a dinner kit and frisbeed the rectangular box into the moving trolley. 'I can't just drop everything for a week. Life doesn't work like that.'

'Grandma can look after me.'

'She's not as spritely as she used to be.' He started down the aisle, Lydia pushing and catching the trolley next to him, needling as she went.

'Spritely?'

'It means active, moving about.'

'Spell it.'

'S-p-r-i-t-e-l-y.'

Lydia mouthed along, memorising it. 'I'll behave,' she begged. 'It's a *really big* prize, Dad. You saw the email – there's only seven people playing. Plus, I've watched all their videos. They're crazy. And *rich*. That's why they're popular, because of their insane prizes! There could be, like, a new car, or even some money, even if you don't win the whole thing. They throw stuff in. That's how it works.'

'I still can't believe they're popular enough to offer something like—'

'They have *ten million* subscribers, Dad.' She said the number like it meant something.

'I don't fancy being watched by ten million people,' Ryan protested. 'Besides, you're forgetting I have work.'

'You hate your job, though.'

Another simple truth, plainly spoken. Ryan considered teaching her some vulgarities, just to take the edge off.

'I don't *hate* my job,' he said, starting to scan their haul through the self-serve check-out. Lydia blipped through the occasional item beside him. 'It's just different these days.'

That was one of those lies parents have to tell their kids to keep up the sunny artifice, but it was a lie he told himself, too. He did hate his job. Loathed it, in fact. He'd worked his way up the ladder, he'd hauled the shit, he'd done his time, earned his stripes. And now, well, he was back to where he'd started. It had seemed an easy – and right – decision at the time to leave his job and spend every remaining second he could with Rita. And, while he wouldn't have changed that decision for anything, it was also true that he hadn't put much thought into the *starting again* part after she died. He'd thought his savings would last them at least a couple of years, but unexpected bills are good friends with terminal illnesses. And when did funerals get so expensive? The funeral directors had no shame in tearing slips from a tear-blotted chequebook. And once they were through all that, a global virus was perfectly timed with a job search for an executive chef with a two-year gap in his résumé. The bills kept coming. Corporate sympathy amounted to putting him on a 'hardship payment plan', which was no better than a fourth credit card, accumulating debt in the background, while the stamps on the envelopes he received changed colour from yellow to orange to red.

One job, at last, came through a friend of a friend, like a tossed coin into a busker's cap: pouring beers at 3 a.m. in a local gambling lounge. It was just supposed to be for a little while, an easy job where he could put his feet up, read a couple of novels during the night shift and keep the wolf from his door at the same time. Just for a little while.

The popularity of the slot machines had surprised him. If the pandemic had shown anyone anything, it was that, when push came to shove, the people above you will protect their lifestyles by trapping you in yours. People wanted shortcuts, they watched a future filled with debt balloon and the picket-fence dream rot in front of them, and they started looking harder for a golden ticket. Ryan watched the stream of hopefuls pouring their wallets into the machines every night. They were searching for a win, sure, but most of them were searching for a ticket *out*. He watched people spend their last dollar on that chance, the neon lights of the machines making their tired faces gaunt, safe in his moral superiority that he wasn't like them, guarded by the fake wooden panelling of the bar, as he poured them their next drink.

One night, the flashing lights and clamour of bells announced that one of his regulars had won a jackpot – seventeen grand. The man had stumbled over to Ryan, ordered a rum and Coke and tipped him a hundred-dollar note. It was the worst tip Ryan had ever got, not that he knew it at the time. On the surface he was stunned and grateful, but, underneath, *something* had detonated in his subconscious. He didn't even realise he'd walked a different route home until he was in front of a different club, thinking that he might like to buy a ticket for himself.

It wasn't difficult to hide, seeing as he worked nights. He'd sorted his routine: work until dawn close, then mosey up the road to the all-nighter and be home before Lydia woke up. Gambling paid his wage at one bar and then reeled it back in at the next. Pretty soon, that wasn't enough. He started borrowing. From people who didn't send letters. Who'd never heard the phrase 'hardship payment plan'.

Four months later and Mr Jackpot, Mr Seventeen-Grand, was back in Ryan's bar, begging for a free drink – *Remember, I tipped you that hundred, you ungrateful prick!* – and sitting in front of the same machine that was supposed to have changed his life four months ago.

Ryan walked the long way home that night, past the second club. He dawdled out the front, moth to the neon and the jangling carnival tunes, but he didn't go inside. He still walked the long way home every night, though. Because he knew he'd have to work his bar, to chip away at the debts he owed both to those who sent letters and to those who didn't, and he'd see the bells and whistles and temptation every night. So now he wanted to walk right past the front doors of the other club, every night, so he'd know he'd beaten it. Though some nights, he'd admit, he stood closer to the door than others.

What Lydia was begging him to do – the gameshow she'd applied for him to be a part of, and the fact that *he*, out of thousands of applicants, had been selected – sounded like one of those tickets out. And Ryan didn't believe in tickets anymore.

As they finished scanning the groceries, he checked the screen, but the total was off. That confused him for a second. He'd carefully picked the discounted items, and his running tally was rarely wrong. He hit the attendant call button – he was long past feeling embarrassed about calling over a staff member for a couple of cents – but then he saw some shiny foil in their meagre pile. Ryan held it out to Lydia, frowning.

'I thought we could share it,' she said meekly, looking at her shoes.

'Sorry, mate, we can't today.' He handed her the Mars bar, then lifted her chin with his finger. 'It's all right, I'm not mad. Just pop it back where you got it.'

The attendant came over and Ryan explained that his daughter was putting back the chocolate, if they could please remove it from their total. He held back a snipe about the ethics of placing a rack of lollies right next to the check-outs, because he figured the employee probably got enough of that. Even though the total was now as he'd expected, his heart still skipped a beat while holding his credit card up to the reader, waiting for the beep of approval. Adrenaline junkies didn't need to jump out of planes, he thought, they could just try to buy some shit they're not sure they can afford. It's the same rush.

A man dressed as an Indian guru was levitating out the front of the supermarket. The performer, a white man in borderline racist make-up, had his legs crossed a metre and a half off the ground, one arm waving through the air alongside some tantric music coming from a mini-speaker underneath him. His other arm was fully extended, gripping onto a pole, with which he was effortlessly holding up his whole body weight. A neat trick.

Ryan, still walking, felt Lydia's weight snag his arm like an anchor as she stopped to gawk at the man. The sun was setting and Ryan checked his watch, calculating the shrinking time he had to get her home, fed and tucked in, before slinking out for his shift until dawn. He hated that he had to leave her overnight – she was only twelve – but he couldn't find any other solution. He knew if anyone found out, he'd be in serious trouble. Child Protective Services had already given him one pass as he'd proved he was working off his debt – the one they were aware of anyway – but he knew he was on notice. If they suspected his daughter was alone six nights a week, or the true scale of what he owed and who he owed it to, he knew they'd take her.

'Dad, got any coins?' Lydia was looking at the guru's turban on the ground, loose change inside.

'Sorry, honey, we have to get going.' Ryan tugged gently at her arm, giving an apologetic grimace to the floating guru, who rolled his eyes in a very un-guru-like manner. Then Ryan saw a tiny corner of foil poking out from Lydia's jacket pocket. 'Lydia, what's in your pocket?'

Her face drained of colour and her eyes bugged. She stuffed her hands in her pockets and spun away from him.

Ryan asked her again, and she shamefully produced the chocolate bar. He shook his head, sighing. 'You know that's wrong.'

Lydia nodded slowly. Sniffed.

'We'll go back together, okay?'

The guru, misreading the situation, said, in an offensive accent not deserving of a donation, 'Go on, man. Let the kid give a dollar.'

Ryan didn't know where the outburst came from. Maybe he was just tired of arguing with his daughter, maybe he was tired of not being able to give her everything she wanted, even something as small as a chocolate bar or the fun of putting some coins in a hat or even, some days, a smile. Maybe he was just tired, period.

'It's fake, okay?' Ryan said to Lydia, pointing at the hand the guru was holding the pole with. 'That arm's made of wood or plaster or something, and there's a rod that goes up his sleeve and latches onto a brace across his shoulder, which holds up the platform he's sitting on. All right? So no, we can't give him a coin.'

'What the hell, man?' The fake accent was gone, now pure Texan drawl. 'You tell her Santa isn't real, too? Get out of here. You're costing me business.'

Ryan strode back towards the shop's entranceway, Lydia sulking behind. A few paces were enough to de-steam him, and he slowed to let Lydia catch up. He knelt in front of her.

'I know it seems like I'm being mean, but you don't just get things you want for free. That's called a shortcut, and even if it looks easy at the time, there're consequences later on. Give me the chocolate. I won't tell anyone. I'll say it's my fault and pretend I forgot to scan it. Just this time. Okay?'

'Mum would've—'

'That's not fair and you know it, love.'

'If you won the competition, we could—' she started.

'Life's not about winning things,' he said, and this time he wasn't just spouting parenting phrases, he believed it. He believed life wasn't about feeding notes into a box filled with flashing lights and praying for a ticket out. That had been a difficult lesson to swallow, but one he'd learned all the same. 'You get what you deserve and you deserve what you get. Everything that comes for free, you end up paying for.'

Even as he was saying it, he thought: *when did you get so jaded?* The chime of coins dropped into a turban mixed with the sound of laughter, from a mother and a young boy, behind them. No, maybe not just jaded. *When did you get so lame?* He shook off the doubt, finished his thought: 'Life's about working hard. You've got to earn things.'

'Maybe,' Lydia sniffled. She held out the chocolate. 'But it seems like you work the hardest out of anyone.' She didn't say it, but he could tell what she was thinking as he took it from her: *and we have the least.*

TWO

Ryan had spent his shift distracted, upset that he'd left Lydia the way he had for the night, upset that he'd had to leave her for the night *at all*, and by morning he was determined that she would never look at him with such baleful, disappointed eyes again.

On the other hand, was he so scared of losing her that he was doing what was right for *him* and not what was right for her? His interest was outweighing his payments. He'd asked for extra shifts but there were none to give. How long could he stay on this hamster wheel?

There had been a man at the end of the bar since midnight, pouring his troubles over ice. Always bourbon, no variation. He'd signalled Ryan over with a two-fingered salute every hour. He wore a sharp suit and looked like someone who had heavy-enough pockets to need a belt, which meant the policy was to open him a tab in the hope he'd move to the slots. Normally such a barnacle would want to chew Ryan's ear, but this man just kept raising his fingers on the hour and otherwise kept quiet. It meant Ryan had time to himself.

And so he'd opened the acceptance email from the competition and re-read it. It was laden with all of the usual red flags of a scam attempt: *congratulations*, *opportunity of a lifetime*, and *life-changing prize*. He'd looked up the group on YouTube too. Lydia was right, the CashSmashers, as they were called, were a group of video creators with an astounding number of views on their videos. All three had a generic late-teenage heartthrob look that made them all quite photogenic and completely forgettable at the same time. They posed in every thumbnail with their arms folded. With their slight British lilt, even though they were clearly not British, the three of them could have been a boy band. Ryan could almost smell the hairspray through his phone screen.

Their videos fell into a few categories: playing video games, pranks on their friends, brand endorsements and, by far the most popular, outlandish stunts in which they gave away huge prizes to everyday people. Their most popular, titled 'People Fight over Money in the Streets!', had them rigging bags of cash with GoPro cameras and tiny parachutes, lobbing them out of a helicopter and filming the people they floated down to in the middle of Chicago. It had the production values of a Tom Cruise action film, with buzzing helicopters and soaring cityscapes. The video had an addictive quality, a mix of both inspiring generosity – one bag landed beside a single mother as she waited for a tow truck, in a moment that was almost too good to be scripted; another was shared by a group of teenagers having a picnic in a park – and sheer train-wreck curiosity, like when a neon-clad jogger pushed a man in a suit into a river over another bag.

Another popular video, titled 'Last One to Leave', featured a group of people holding onto a luxury car, with the person who stayed touching it the longest driving away in it. The woman who came second had broken down in tears, having to withdraw when her arm started convulsing.

The list went on: 'We paid this boss $100,000 to fire his employee! If he does it, the employee gets DOUBLE!', 'We pretended to steal people's cars in front of them, crashed them, and then gave them a new Mercedes!' Some of the early videos had prizes such as iPods or PlayStations. As the prizes got bigger and the views went up, the situations got crazier. Ryan had no idea how they'd got legal clearance to drop bags of money into a busy city, especially when it started fights. Maybe they hadn't.

Ryan didn't know the equation for how many views accounted for how much income, but he knew some people earned an insane living from YouTube, *and* he knew that the CashSmashers had dropped twenty bags in that stunt, each containing fifty thousand dollars. The bags had the logo of an online gambling company printed on their sides. Given these guys had ten million followers and major sponsorship, Ryan started to wonder if the competition might be legitimately life-changing after all. And, despite himself (*no tickets!*), he started to think that one in seven was pretty good odds . . .

It was nearing dawn. The man at the bar stood, clearing his throat loudly. Ryan moved across the bar to settle the tab, but the man turned his back and walked towards the exit.

'Your tab, buddy,' Ryan called after him. The man was composed enough, his suit well pressed and his behaviour so far genteel enough that Ryan gave him the benefit of the doubt, figuring that he'd simply forgotten.

The man turned and pointed to an envelope on the bar. The envelope was thick. Too thick to be cash, unless the man was a very generous tipper.

'You might take care of the tab for me,' the man said.

Ryan didn't try to stop him leaving. He didn't even need to tip the envelope out on the bar to know what was in it, but he did it anyway. The familiar gloss of photographs shone back at him. There were dozens of them, taken in all different places and at all different times – shops, cinemas, playgrounds, morning, afternoon, night – but all with a singular focus. Lydia.

As the day shift came in, he asked his supervisor if he could cash in all of his annual leave for a week off. It wasn't well received, given the short notice and his previous request for extra shifts, but he stood his ground. He'd be paying for it when he came back. *If* he came back. He used the office printer to sign and scan the indemnity waiver included with the competition invitation, pausing only momentarily at the phrase 'The contestant agrees to accept the risks involved with the competition, including injury and/or death', and emailed back his acceptance.

Getting home, he'd made Lydia pack for her grandmother's without telling her why, leaving his announcement until they'd gotten in the car. She nearly launched out of the sunroof with excitement. As far as apologies went, it was pretty good. He wished Rita was here to see it.

Suddenly everything – his looming debt, the fear of losing Lydia to welfare, the envelope of photographs, the mysterious competition – seemed irrelevant. Her excitement, the idolisation in her eyes, was enough to put any doubts to the back of his mind. If only for a second.

THREE

At every point – as the flight steward scanned his boarding pass, as the hotel concierge tapped in his reservation number, as the cab driver the next morning confirmed the ride had been paid for – Ryan expected a computer to chime, for the attendant to shake their head and tell him he'd been sent on a wild goose chase all along. Being whisked across the country, essentially blindfolded as to where he was really going or how long he was going for, didn't feel real. He was waiting for something to bring him crashing back to reality.

Nothing did. The cab driver dropped him at a *Road Closed* sign at the base of a beachside suburb where the houses rose uphill from golden sand to a small peninsula bordered with majestic cliffs. It was the type of place where the already narrow streets were further cramped by monstrous Range Rovers parked along both sides, and even if you collected every bag of cash the CashSmashers parachuted into Chicago, you wouldn't get a say at an auction. The houses were a mix of old-fashioned brick homes, unrenovated, and modern monstrosities that were rigid, square, and ninety per cent glass. Everything had a second storey with an ocean view. Even from the street, he could hear the waves crashing into the base of cliffs.

Walking up the hill, Ryan still didn't know the rules of the competition he was entering. He knew that the prize was supposed to be *life-changing*. He knew that he was one of seven contestants. He knew what the CashSmashers had given away in their other videos. He'd also learned the hard way that if it sounded too good to be true, it probably was; that you get what you deserve and you deserve what you get. But that didn't stop his stomach fluttering as he walked past a huge black RV, back doors splayed open to reveal a cargo space filled with television screens and broadcasting equipment, the first real sign that what he was walking into was genuine. The road had levelled out now and he could see the ocean, as bright and sparkly as a film crew could ask for. Cresting the hill, the wind tickling him more, he realised that the end of the street was actually the precipice of one of the mighty cliffs. A group of people stood around at the end of the cul-de-sac.

A boy – because that was the only way to describe him (their online bios said all the CashSmashers were 'in their twenties', but Ryan had a feeling that was their real age plus tax) – spotted Ryan and ran up to him. He was holding a video camera that he couldn't keep still, the screen flipped so he could see it but the lens pointed back at himself, a bright light and fuzzy microphone fixed to the top. He wore a cap with *CashSmashers* written on it in a font that looked like a graffiti tag, and a baggy hoody, despite the bright sun, with the same logo. He started talking without saying hello.

'And here we have our fifth contestant!' He was bouncing up and down, wobbling the camera everywhere, like he was filming a guerrilla skateboarding video, walking as he did so. His entire personality seemed to be energy drinks. Ryan tried to keep in step, but it was basically a jog. 'Ryan Jay . . . Jay . . .' The boy stopped jigging up and down, filtered the Red Bull out of his voice and said quietly, 'How do you say it, dude?'

'Jaegan,' Ryan said, pronouncing the soft J, unsure whether to talk to the boy's face or the camera in his hand.

'Ryan Jaegan, everyone!' The Red Bull was back. It was like every sentence was hosting a gameshow: *come on dooooown*. He was exhausting to listen to. 'Tell us why you're here.'

'Um, hi, everybody,' Ryan gave a wave to the camera and felt like an idiot.

'It's not live, dude.' The kid's energy switched off again.

'Oh, okay.'

'Ryan Jaegan, everyone! Tell us why you're here.' He said it as if he'd never said it the first time.

'My, ah, my daughter filled in the application for me.' Then, knowing it would make him a suck-up, Ryan added, 'She loves you guys.'

'Aw, that's sweet. And it's just you and her, isn't it? Single dad. That's pretty cool.'

'My wife . . . er . . . passed away a few years ago,' Ryan stammered. He shouldn't have been surprised they knew this much, but it still shook him. He immediately regretted saying anything about Rita; he knew how cruel the internet would be. But then again, while he hated all the reality TV shows, Rita and Lydia used to watch them in secret. She might have been excited he was here, he decided. He spun his wedding ring, which he still wore in her memory, around his finger. It was enough to stop him turning around and leaving.

'Ouch. Bummer, dude,' the youngster interrupted.

Ryan just shrugged. It wasn't how he'd put it, but it wasn't wrong either. Yeah, actually, he decided, that sums up my life pretty well: *Bummer, dude.*

'Aaaall riiiight!' the boy said. 'Welcome to CashSmashers, Ryan. I'm Lucas. I've just got one more question for you. Are you ready to . . .'—he started slapping his knee with his spare hand, like a drum roll—'smash. That. Caaaaash?'

'I guess so.'

The boy looked nonplussed, as if he was expecting a different reply.

Ryan shrugged. 'Oh, sorry, do you have a catchphrase I'm supposed to use or something?'

'Great, okay.' The boy lowered the camera and his voice dropped an octave, muttering to himself as he shielded himself from the sun with one hand and re-watched the footage, wrinkling his nose as he did so. 'I think that's all right, actually. We could take it again, but I kinda like you as an underdog. The whole awkward boomer thing works for you.'

'I'm thirty-eight.'

'Oh.' The boy scanned him, trying to figure out if anyone over twenty-five was a boomer, while processing how a thirty-eight-year-old could be a widower, and realising that it could only be a combination of bad breaks and worse luck. 'Shit.'

'Yeah,' Ryan said. 'Bummer, dude.'

But the boy had stopped paying attention. He'd spied someone else coming up the hill and sprinted off. Ryan heard in the distance: *and heeeere coooomes contestant number six!*

FOUR

It wasn't hard to tell the contestants from the crew, just from the look of confusion on their faces. If you could call a bunch of teenagers with handheld video cameras a production crew, that is; it seemed like the three CashSmashers were doing everything themselves. Ryan supposed the whole DIY thing was part of their brand; there was no other reason people worth this much money wouldn't have an army of assistants running around. He was surprised to find himself respecting that, just a little.

Six contestants were gathered at the end of the road. It was a motley group. There was a bubbly young woman who was clearly a fan of the YouTubers, black hair straightened and make-up carefully done, ready to be seen by millions, and with so many ear piercings she risked compression in her neck. A middle-aged woman who had an impatient scowl, one hand in the pocket of her knee-length overcoat, and who Ryan felt looked familiar but couldn't place. A primly dressed Asian-American woman in a white blouse with a pencil skirt; Ryan had gambled that there might be some physical aspect to the competition, so had worn a T-shirt and loose-fitting jeans, and he hoped for this woman's sake he was wrong.

A wavy-haired Black man who looked like a surfer in fluorescent boardshorts and a singlet, lying on the warm asphalt, seemingly to pass the time. And last, a near-seven-foot giant who looked like an athlete. Lucas and his two pals were further down the street, checking their smart watches, presumably waiting for number seven.

Ryan introduced himself to the athlete, purely because he was tall enough to be a landmark to get his bearings from, and was met with a gruff, 'The name's Ned.' As they shook hands, the middle-aged woman approached and told Ryan her name was Michelle. She didn't shake, both her hands stuffed in her pockets for warmth. It was a bright morning, but the wind kicked off the cliff edge in a way that cut the air with cold. 'I'm not sure who we're waiting for, but I hope they're penalised,' she said. 'Invite said we started at midday sharp. As far as I'm concerned, they shouldn't play.'

Ned shrugged, not seeming to mind the wait. His voice was as deep as his physique had suggested. 'Play?'

'I know as much as you do. It's more exciting if we figure this out on the fly rather than coming prepared. But there's a prize, so I assume there's a winner,' Michelle explained.

Ryan had a fleeting thought that if this was a competition, it might be good to take this early opportunity to size up potential alliances, but no one else seemed to be and he didn't want to appear too competitive in case it made him a target.

Ned beat him to it. 'If it's a voting-people-out thing, I say we put our first one to the late guy. Or girl. It's only fair.'

Ryan gave a noncommittal nod, hopefully enough to keep him on side with both of them but not committing too much to anything. There was no point strategising until he knew the rules of whatever 'game' he was getting into.

He made some excuse about having a look around and walked aimlessly over to the end of the road, where a small rocky plateau led to a wooden deck lookout. On either side was a flimsy wire fence adorned with signs that had a little stick figure slipping atop crumbling rocks, an oddly comical way to warn someone of the risk of instant death. A house across the street had a few peering faces smudging the front windows, wondering what was going on. On the other side of the street was a much more lavish home, only partially visible behind a huge black iron gate. Ryan could see a sandstone driveway, so long it had a turning circle with a fountain in the middle of it at the end. He wandered out onto the lookout to get a better view of the sea-facing real estate.

The clifftop mansion was impressive. It had a bulbous, convex-windowed living area that from above must look like a wheel. The curved windows jutted out from the rest of the house, not over the cliff as such, but over the jungle of a garden below, which was carved into the cliffside either side of a set of rocky stairs. A much smaller window was lodged between vines, as if it had been built *into* the rock. Beyond the glass living room, he could see the glint of an infinity pool, the glass precipice with no discernible edge making it look like you'd be swimming in the air. Ryan leaned over the railing slightly to get a better a look inside the living area, seeing pure white carpet (a luxury for people who can afford to *clean* pure white carpet, he thought) and a large black object in the centre of the room. He couldn't see it properly, so he leaned a bit further over the edge.

A sudden hand on his shoulder gave him a push.

FIVE

Ryan looked down, at least four storeys to the waves below. Vertigo rocked him. He straightened up and whirled around. The pencil-skirt woman had both her hands in the air, an embarrassed grimace on her face.

'Whoa, sorry,' she gushed. 'I was going to make a joke about how you'd better watch out, you never know who might tip you over for the prize. Bad taste, I know. I regretted it as soon as I pushed you. My name's May.' She held out a hand. 'Can we do introductions and apologies at the same time?'

'Sure.' He shook her hand. 'Ryan. Sorry, I might have overreacted. It was only a little nudge.'

'I did try to murder you.'

'In broad daylight, with cameras around.' He nodded back towards the RV. 'That's a confident murderer.'

'I'm trying not to notice the cameras, to be honest. If I know someone's watching me, I clam right up. I came to say hi because you look like the most normal person here, not to throw you off a cliff. I'm not into all this stuff. I'm here under duress, you could say. You look like you might be the same.'

'You got me.' Ryan found himself relaxing, relieved that there was another person sort of like him here. Though he doubted her definition of duress was quite the same as his. And if it was, was she seeking an early ally? He decided he was overthinking the game. 'My daughter filled in the application for me,' he said.

'Cute! My best friend applied but I was in her application video, to help her out with questions, and they chose me instead. Can you believe it? They wrote to her and said, "Thanks, but who's the hot chick behind you?"' She scoffed. 'Not in those words, of course, but I could tell. My friend was absolutely *livid*. I wanted to say no, but she wouldn't let me. Besides, I'm a psychologist – whatever this is, I figure it will be an interesting experiment at least. Maybe I can write a paper on it afterwards.'

Her answer appeared relaxed and honest. Ryan reminded himself to not get carried away with the competition of it all. 'Sounds like your best friend and my daughter would get along. Well, good to meet you, May. Hey, check it out.' He pointed. Something was happening back at the main group. It looked like the seventh con-testant had arrived.

Ryan and May headed back to the others. The new member was the youngest of the group, cheeks pocked with acne scars and a patchy black participation-award of a beard. He was wearing navy blue hospital scrubs.

There was a loud whining buzz. Ryan looked around but he couldn't see where it was coming from. He wondered if it was part of the contest.

'New guy's the one to watch,' Michelle whispered. It took Ryan a moment to realise she was talking to him. 'He's going for visual storytelling, wearing his uniform so everyone watching quickly knows who he is. You need a story. They have to remember *our* names, but he's *the doctor*. It'll get him on screen more and, if it's audience-voted, he'll have an advantage.'

May leaned in. 'You obviously know a lot about these kinds of things.' She said it as a statement, but Michelle knew it was a question. Michelle shot Ryan a sceptical glance that asked *can we trust her*, as if their alliance was being intruded upon.

'I like gameshows,' Michelle said.

Ryan suddenly remembered where he recognised her from. One of the CashSmashers' videos – he just couldn't quite remember which one. She was a returning player. That made sense; reality shows always liked to bring back the favourites. 'Well, I'm here for my daughter. That's my story.'

'That's a good one. You're here to fill the family-man arc.'

'What does that make yours? Redemption?' He suddenly remembered which video he'd seen her in. 'You just missed out on winning that car, didn't you?'

Michelle laughed. 'So you saw that?'

Ryan nodded, recalling Michelle's arm literally spasming with cramps as she let go of the sportscar, bursting into tears at second place.

Michelle shook her head at the memory. 'That was a tough one. My arm hurt for *weeks*.'

'So you know how these things work. Do you know what they've got in store for us?'

'We all know what they do, but they like to hide what we're here to win and how we're supposed to win it. I think I have some idea, if I had to bet.' She nodded to the front, where the three boys looked as if they were about to either break into song or film some more footage. Lucas was doing the filming selfie-style again. Ryan was grateful Lucas was holding the video camera, otherwise it would have been difficult to tell the three apart, with their cookie-cutter private-school skateboarder looks. They all wore black T-shirts with their logo, which was supposed to look like graffiti, on the front and the gambling company on the back. Ryan tried to spot the differences between them. One was tall, with a beanie tight on his head, coils of hair spilling out from under it. A shorter one was playing with what looked like a video-game controller. And there was Lucas.

That buzz again. Ryan looked up, and realised it was coming from a drone flying above them.

'Hello, Smashers!' the tall one in the beanie yelled. 'Welcome to our biggest video yet!' He emphasised each word.

Michelle whooped and hollered. Ryan gently clapped along, not wanting to seem too much of a killjoy, but not yet shameless.

'None of you know what you're competing for just yet, all you know is that the prize is guaranteed to be *life-changing*.'

The shorter boy pushed his face into the camera. 'And let me tell you, this prize is cah-razy. It's the most hugest thing we've ever given away and one of these seven'—Lucas did a spin to capture them all—'is going to win it.'

'All right, everyone.' Beanie-kid was back in centre frame. He lifted a little gadget with a button on it, like a small remote control, above his head. 'It's my pleasure to announce that the prize you are competing for is worth *four million dollars*.'

The group immediately started whispering together. May nudged Ryan and raised her eyebrows, as if to say: *this can't be real*. Ryan wondered what else might be in the truck. Actually, he wondered what on earth could be worth that much money. He decided that Beanie-kid must be being hyperbolic. They were chasing clicks and views, after all. 'So now you know what the prize is worth, it's time to tell you what you're playing for. And then we'll tell you how to win it. One of you lucky seven will win . . .' Beanie-kid held the remote in the air and hit the button. Nothing happened for a second, and then slowly, in front of the clifftop mansion, the pair of black iron gates started to rumble open.

SIX

They filed into the driveway, necks set to swivel, as the manic hosts led them towards the house. A vine-snaked wall separated the front courtyard from the street and the cliffs, curving around to protect the complex from the road and the weather. To Ryan's left was a double garage; to his right, along the coastal wall, was a set of stairs that, he knew already, descended into a garden, safely carved into the cliffside like a balcony. There was no upper storey, which was probably the only thing keeping another million off the price tag, but who needed elevation in a place like this? Even just a few steps onto the drive, the house felt sheltered, the noise of the wind replaced by the bubbling of the fountain and the drone buzzing in the background as it zipped around in the air. Ryan was sure it wasn't intentional, but when Beanie-kid pressed the button again and the gate clanked shut behind them, it felt a bit like they were being sealed in.

The front door had a vertical metal handle, like a fridge. Lucas opened it with familiar theatricality and ran inside, pivoting to get footage of everyone filing in. Everything was white: white-painted walls and plush white carpet, which was just as soft underfoot as Ryan had expected it to be. The boys led them to the right, oceanward, through a surprisingly narrow corridor. Ryan took a glance to his left: there were two closed doors and one open one, through which he saw a blindingly clean marble-tiled bathroom. As they made their way down the corridor, all the rest of the doors were closed – including, Ryan supposed, one to the basement level, as there wasn't a staircase in sight.

Just when Ryan was thinking that maybe the whole place was cramped and overvalued, the corridor expanded into a sunken open-plan living space, magnificently spacious and brightly lit, helped primarily by the 270 degrees of windows. On the platform where Ryan was standing was an ornately carved oak table, better suited for a boardroom than a dinner party, and a stainless-steel kitchen behind him with all the trimmings, including a fancy art-deco knife block inside a niche, and a marble island. A black rectangular box sat on the island. Bordering the corridor wall was a bar, with a counter someone could bartend behind, lined with silver Canopic-looking jars, and a glass-panelled cabinet mounted to the wall, better stocked than the back shelves of most pubs. The opposite wall had a sliding door, leading to the infinity pool that, now Ryan was closer, really did look like it was gently lapping over the edge of the cliff.

The main attraction, the windowed circular pit, was irresistible. Two plush white steps led down to where it felt like you were almost floating in the air. Everything in the 'pit' was also designed in a circle: there was a circular white leather sofa surrounding a cast iron fireplace – the black object Ryan had seen from outside – where a small fire crackled, enough to warm the room to uncomfortable. Ryan suspected it was only lit to make the room look sophisticated on film. A black sports bag, zipped up, sat in between the couch and the fireplace, marooned and out of place in this pristine oasis. There wasn't even a TV.

Perhaps that was downstairs, Ryan thought. Or maybe you

didn't need one with the view. He wouldn't know; he'd never had a proper view before. His and Rita's first apartment was sandwiched mid-level between two towering office blocks – close enough to the ground to hear the garbage trucks all night, but not high enough to see over the offices. The only view they'd ever had was from her hospital window, which looked out to the ocean. Ryan felt the familiar pang, looking around this dream house, of wanting to share it with her. If she'd been here, he'd have done anything to win it for her and give her the ocean view she'd deserved.

He noticed small grey boxes with blinking red lights mounted at intervals on the roof. Cameras. Probably with a direct feed to the RV outside.

Drone-kid had headed out to the deck surrounding the pool and started piloting the drone in a vertical hover around the outside of the glass living room. The contestants had stopped whispering to each other; half were probably in awe of the house, while the other half were plotting how to win it. The surfer had taken a relaxed seat on the steps into the pit, legs spread like he was the kind of substitute teacher who started lessons by saying *now, I'm not your usual substitute*. Lucas jumped on the leather couch with a level of disregard that only a teenager with four million dollars to do away with could possess. Beanie-kid ushered those still milling around in the kitchen down into the pit, and then handed around a lock box for them to drop their phones into. Ryan sent a quick love-heart emoji to Lydia, then turned it off and dropped it in. Beanie-kid put the lock box down and then leapt like Fred Astaire onto the couch.

'All right, Brayden,' said Lucas, giving Beanie-kid, who Ryan now realised was the ringleader, the thumbs up. 'You're good.'

'I hope you all like what you've seen, but don't worry, you'll have *plenty* of time to explore the place,' Brayden said. 'Now, I can't dangle four mill in front of you and not tell you how to win it. So,' he lowered his voice almost conspiratorially, 'listen closely.'

SEVEN

'Here are the rules.'

He paused to build the suspense. Everyone was deathly quiet.

'First, you must all pick a hand. Then, in about . . .' Brayden checked his smart watch and then sucked air through his teeth as he calculated, 'five minutes-ish, place that hand on one of the walls of this house. From there, there's only one more rule. You can do whatever you want, move around as much as you like – but if you take your hand off the house, *for any reason, at any time*, you're out. The last person to let go wins *the house*. Property value: four million big ones. It's a Last One to Leave competition!'

He spread his arms like he was expecting another excited round of applause. He didn't receive it; everyone was looking around, thinking it through. Ryan noticed Michelle was glowing: this was the game she'd played before, for the car. She was ready for it.

A slight scowl flickered across Brayden's face at the lack of enthusiasm, but he quickly hid it – Ryan assumed because he'd remembered they were filming – instead saying in his best hosting voice, 'Do you have questions or something?' It was clear he thought it was ridiculous he had to ask.

The young doctor – though up-close Ryan was sure he was too young to be a real doctor – raised his hand. 'Do the windows count as well as walls?'

'Yes. Windows count. Anything vertical plays.'

'Can we swap hands?' Ned, the athlete, asked.

'No. The one you pick to start with is the one you have to keep in contact the entire time.'

'Can we go outside?' May chipped in.

Brayden looked over at Lucas, who just shrugged. Ryan realised they were making most of the rules up on the fly. His question about how they'd legally managed to drop bags of cash into a busy city lunch hour had answered itself: they pulled the stunt first and asked questions later.

'Sure. Fine. Yep. If you're still touching a wall, you can go outside.'

'What about food and water?' That was the young doctor again.

'We'll provide food. The taps work. There're glasses in the fridge.' Brayden was agitated now, speaking quickly.

'Are we allowed to touch each other?' That was the woman who'd dressed up for the filming, who Ryan had thought was a fan of the group. She said it thoughtfully, slower than the other questions, as though everyone else was clarifying the rules and she was dissecting them, thinking of a shortcut to winning.

'Of course not.'

'Like, with permission, though?'

'Well . . . sure. You can't push anyone off, though. If you do that we'll eliminate you, and they can stay in, okay?'

The woman shrugged as though she hadn't really cared about the answer anyway.

The surfer yawned, cricked his neck theatrically, stood up and walked through the middle of the group to the furthest section of the living room, where the view was uninterrupted sky and ocean. He took his left hand, blew a puff of air into it and placed it flat, with a firm slap, on the window. He raised his eyebrows to the rest of them: *game on*.

Brayden allowed himself a smile, which was cut off with another question from the doctor.

'Does it have to be the whole hand or like, just a . . .'

'Jesus Christ!' Brayden snapped. 'Put your hand on the wall, don't take it off. What's so hard about that? Just, like, play fair.'

Ryan thought it was funny that they would put such a whopping prize in front of a group of strangers and ask them to play fair, but he kept his snickering to himself. He heard a snort from May beside him, also trying to hold it in. He decided, if he needed an ally, she'd be a good one.

'Fingertips are fine,' Lucas said, finally relieving his friend. 'Anything past the wrist really, no matter how small the contact is. We've got cameras in the roof and we'll be watching from out front when we're not in here with you. They cover all the angles pretty well, plus we'll be around and, of course, even if you think a camera hasn't caught you, your new friends are probably going to rat on you.' He gave a *not much I can do about it* grimace. 'It's worth four million dollars after all. Watch your backs.'

'You don't have cameras in the bathroom, do you?' Ryan asked.

There was a murmur of interest.

'Ah.' Brayden finally had a question they'd thought through beforehand. 'There is one camera—'

He was cut off by a roar of dissent.

All those windows amplified the sound so that the argument sounded more like a music festival in full swing. Everyone was trying to raise their voice above everyone else's, and the murmur of concern quickly turned into full-blown yelling.

Brayden eventually got them under control. 'Hang on, hang on, *hang on!* There is a black line on the toilet wall above all the'— he spun a hand while he tried to find a word—'*action*. So our camera is framed above that. It captures nothing else in that room, so your privacy is safe. You have to keep your hand above that line, though, in view of the camera, or you're out.'

That seemed to satisfy everyone. Ryan tried to think of any further questions. He didn't know much about gameshows, but he assumed they normally had regulatory licences, rules of fair play and, no doubt, insurance, at least for those big ones where people go into the jungle or live in a house together. But thinking it through only reaffirmed his theory that these three boys, teenagers with bank statements that must read like phone numbers, had probably skipped a few of the more mundane legalities. Still, it didn't really matter if they were idiots, did it? An idiot giving away a house is still giving away a house. Hell, it's probably preferable.

'What about the shower?' the surfer called from across the room, surprising Ryan with a slight French accent. Ryan had assumed from the look of him that he'd care the least about showering, so he was probably just enjoying needling the hosts.

Brayden chewed his lip. 'You're trying to win four million dollars – skip the damn shower. Look at that'—he checked his smart watch—'after that delightful chat, you've got sixty seconds until we start.'

Ryan suspected Brayden's watch wasn't set to any particular time; he just wanted to shut everyone up. But it worked. The doctor, on hearing this, sprinted up the hall, which seemed an odd starting move. Ned and the superfan both walked to opposite sides of the pit and chose a window panel each. Ned wore a wedding band, which made a *chink* on the glass. Superfan flexed her fingers, cracked her wrists and placed a single pointed fingertip delicately on her chosen window. Michelle looked around and settled on the intersection of the window and a stylish metal feature section of the wall, and sat down next to it. It looked uncomfortable – there were lots of little jags and grooves – but maybe she thought it would be less slippery

than glass. Ryan noticed that Michelle chose the hand she'd kept
in her pocket, and that she was wearing a glove. She'd mentioned
having an inkling of what was in store for them all, and she'd been
pleased when Brayden had announced the style of competition,
as if it was just as she'd hoped. She certainly looked like she was
prepared: resting her hand first, then keeping it covered for warmth.
She was obviously the one to beat. Despite the glove, a ring she was
wearing made a heavy *clunk* on the wall, sounding heavier than
Ned's simple band: probably some kind of gaudy jewellery.

Ryan hadn't moved yet. He was wondering whether it was better
to use his dominant hand, which he could probably hold up for
longer, but would limit what he could do with his spare hand, when
he felt May give him a nudge. She walked up the two steps into the
kitchen, dragged one of the stools from the marble island across to the
nearest wall, perched on it and put her right hand on the splashback
by resting her elbow on the counter and leaning forward. It looked
far more comfortable than standing with an outstretched arm. Ryan
changed his mind about Michelle; maybe *May* was the one to beat . . .

Ryan sighed. It seemed so stupid, but he'd come all the way there.
Whether he believed in tickets out or not, he'd bought one. And he
knew Lydia would be watching. Just like she used to, her mother's
arm around her, a bowl of popcorn between them, discussing who
was the best singer or how not to get voted off an island. He might
as well try. He walked between the surfer and Michelle, where there
was the most room between contestants.

'Ten seconds, everyone.'

A toilet flushed from the hallway. The doctor sprinted in, placing
his right hand – which he'd definitely not had time to wash – on the
wall at the end of the corridor.

'Five seconds.'

Ryan took a deep breath and placed his left hand flat against the
glass.

EIGHT

If you drew lines between the five of them, spread out in the circular pit, leaving out May and the doctor on the platform above, it would form a pentagram.

The CashSmasher flying the drone came inside, the dragonfly-like four-rotored robot tucked under his arm. He took in everyone's position and gave his mates a thumbs up, then walked over to the kitchen island and pressed something on top of the black rectangular box. A series of red digital zeroes sprung to life: a timer.

The three boys made their way to the corridor, fist-pumping as they did so, mugging for the cameras.

'Before we leave you to it, there is one more *tiny* thing,' Brayden said, turning back and pretending he'd just remembered something.

Lucas scurried into a crouch to get a good shot.

'I'm sure you're wondering what's with this.' He pointed to the black sports bag in the middle of the room. Ryan realised it had been placed in the centre on purpose, equidistant from all of the walls and windows, and impossible to reach without taking a hand off the wall. They were offering a trade, a sacrificial choice. 'That bag has fifty thousand dollars in it. Good luck.'

NINE

'So . . . do we just, like . . . stand here?' the doctor asked as the clock ticked over to only the second minute, a warning of the boredom ahead.

'You can take the money if you want it,' Ned said, tilting his head towards the bag. His tone was jokey, but they were all weighing it up: if they weren't likely to win anyway, why not just grab the bag now?

'I saw one of these in Japan,' May said. 'A woman died because she didn't go to the bathroom for three days. And that wasn't even for a house, it was for a video game or something.' She looked around and saw everyone wincing. 'What? It's a true story.'

'There was that show in the UK – we studied it at med school,' the young doctor contributed. 'They wanted to see who could go the longest without sleep. People went *literally* psychotic. The whole show got shut down.'

'Reckon that will happen to us?' Ned scoffed. 'Any psychos among you?'

'If we're all stuck here together for, well, who knows how long, we may as well get to know each other,' Superfan said.

Because of her dozen piercings, her head jangled like a tambourine every time she moved. She was bright, bubbly and clearly comfortable in front of a camera. 'I'll start. My name's Lisa. I run my own beauty vlog on YouTube. My handle is at-Lisa's-Looks.' She said it slowly, and Ryan realised she was hoping there were microphones in the room; she was here for the millions of eyes the CashSmashers usually got on their videos. Free publicity. 'I've been following these guys for a while and thought, hey, that'll be fun. Who's next?'

The surfer started to walk around the circle, trailing his hand across the windows like he was tussling a cornfield, whistling to himself. He reached Ryan first but didn't say anything, just stood next to him and raised an eyebrow. Ryan obliged by ducking, so the surfer could trail his hand above Ryan's head as they crossed over. The surfer kept going, whistling, doing the same to Michelle, before disappearing down the corridor.

'My name's Ryan,' Ryan volunteered, given everyone else's silence. He thought about what Lucas had told him out front – *I like the boomer thing for you* – and decided to play it a bit clueless. 'My daughter applied for me. I don't really know a lot about this stuff, so I'm just giving it a go.'

Michelle went next. 'I've played this, sort of, before, with a car. I didn't win that, but I came second, so looks like they invited me back to try again.' Ryan realised another reason she might have known what the competition would involve: she understood the character arc they had for her. Like the doctor wearing his scrubs: clear and easy to remember.

'I remember that!' Lisa said. 'It was like a Ferrari or something, wasn't it?'

'Aston Martin.'

'Wow. How much are these guys worth?' May asked.

'You wouldn't believe me if I told you,' Lisa said.

'Ten million subscribers. Total views across all videos in the hundreds of millions,' the doctor said.

'Plus sponsors,' May added. Ryan remembered the flying bags of money had been sponsored by a betting company. The same logo was on the back of their T-shirts, so maybe this one had been too. If that was the case, they probably all had betting odds lined up next to their names. It chilled him.

'They can spend a million a video *easy*. But this . . .' Lisa was getting excited, nearly bouncing on the spot. 'This has never been done before, not to this scale. Michelle, how long d'you go for last time? Any tips?'

'Seventy-five hours. Not much I can tell you except that it's boring. And it's harder than it looks – like, physically painful. My elbow still clicks.'

Ryan looked at the timer. He realised it was glowing red at the back, so the numbers were visible on both sides. At six minutes in, the day ahead didn't seem so arduous and he also knew Michelle was probably trying to scare them. Even so, the physical challenge would no doubt be tough – sleep deprivation, muscle cramps – and he'd only just started to realise there was a mental side too: the boredom, the competition. And that was without the additional temptation of the bag of money in the middle of the room. A lot of things could go wrong.

'Adam. I'm a med student,' the young man in scrubs volunteered from the corridor, ducking to let the whistling surfer, who'd made a lap down the other end of the house and started through the kitchen, back through. 'Um, I'm here because I figured it would beat working at McDonald's. Medical degrees aren't cheap, you know.'

May recoiled under the surfer's armpit as he passed her next. Maybe he was right to be concerned about the shower, Ryan thought. 'I'm May. My friend and I applied together, just for fun,' she said. Ryan waited for her to go on, but she kept it there, deliberately leaving out that she'd only been in the background of her friend's audition and had been *asked* to apply. She probably didn't want people to think she was a threat or a favourite. Ryan found himself reassessing her again. She'd also left out that she was a psychologist, and therefore equipped to play mind games. Everyone was just getting warmed up, but she was already playing. In those imaginary online betting odds, he pictured her near the top.

'Ned.' Ned lifted his spare arm in a wave. The surfer had reached him now, but Ned didn't move to let him past, simply shook his head and said, 'Nah, mate.' The surfer shrugged. Ned was too tall for him to pass without his lifting his hand, so he plonked himself down at Ned's feet, like a cat waiting to be fed. 'I'm an electrician.'

Not an athlete, Ryan thought, though he was built like one – perhaps he'd been one in his youth. In any case, Ryan added his physical strength to mental grit and put him near the top of his imagined betting odds too.

'Me and the boys at work thought we'd all apply. I got through, so here I am.' Ned looked down at the surfer in disdain. 'All right, your turn. Name?'

The surfer shook his head and said, 'Nope.'

That stopped the conversation. They all remained silent for a few more agonising minutes. Ryan eventually decided that walking around might help him think everything through and come up with a personal strategy. Besides, the hosts had said they could do whatever they wanted. If there was a bag of cash in the middle of the lounge, there could be anything down the hall. He didn't expect anyone to drop out in the first few hours, but now was the time to figure out all the angles of the game, while he still had a clear head. It would also help him decide if he was going to take the money. He needed it, that was true. And fifty grand was enough to make sure no one dropped any more envelopes full of photos of his daughter at his work. But it wouldn't change his life – *Lydia's* life – the way a house, a home, could. Besides, what would Lydia think if he quit so soon? He needed to weigh that up. He apologetically stepped over Michelle and headed into the corridor.

With his back to the ocean, he knew that the wall to his left bordered the driveway and fountained courtyard. There was one door to his right as he walked back towards the entrance, but he couldn't reach it unless he did a full circuit, as he wasn't allowed to swap hands. He was careful to keep his palm on the wall; he didn't trust just his fingertips to keep in contact with the surface. He felt stupid, but he didn't want to be eliminated on a technicality.

Past the entranceway there was a T-junction, with three doors, one each side and one at the end. He opened the door to his left. The room was empty except for a bed made up with freshly fluffed pillows as if for a real-estate catalogue. It was probably too danger-ous to lie down: he'd either have to keep one hand above his head, touching the wall over the headboard, or lie on his side and extend his arm out to the nearest wall. Doable, sure, but if he nodded off and his arm slipped, he'd be out. There was a blinking red light in the far cornice, another watchful camera. The CashSmashers were clearly expecting these rooms to be used, for everyone to spread out. Ryan walked in and opened the closet. There was a whir and a hiss from inside and a small digital safe spun open. It must have been wired to the cupboard door, to open at the same time.

'Find anything?' May's voice startled him. He turned to see her leaning into the room, her hand gripped around the door frame. She smiled. 'Thought I'd keep you company.'

Or keep an eye on me, Ryan thought, and immediately felt guilty for it. The mind games were indeed starting early.

'I just thought, you know, if there's money in there'—he gestured towards the living space—'there might be something else. Something that helps out.' He looked into the safe. 'Like this!' He pulled out a half-used roll of silver duct tape. He didn't know if it had been left there on purpose as part of the game or the boys just hadn't thought through cleaning the house, but surely super-strength tape would prove useful. The rest of the wardrobe was empty, and there was a camera in the room, so he settled on it being deliberate.

'Is that fair?' May asked. She phrased it gently, but Ryan could tell she was both slightly concerned he might have an advantage and pleased that he'd found it. No, pleased that she'd *seen* him find it.

'I didn't bring it.' Ryan shrugged, looping the roll over his wrist and gesturing to the safe. 'Anyway, this is all keyed up to open on cue. I didn't even have to type in a code. They clearly want it to be part of the game. It might come in handy.' He continued around the room, pulling open the bedside drawers, also empty, meeting up with May at the door. 'Well, at least we know where the beds are.'

'Dangerous,' May said, spare hand squishing a soft pillow. 'I wouldn't risk it.'

By virtue of having approached from the opposite wall of the corridor, May now led the way as Ryan left the first bedroom and continued his circuit. The door at the end of the hall opened into a larger, more luxurious bedroom. All of the cupboards and drawers were stripped bare (or possibly not: Ryan remembered that the nameless surfer and Adam had been down this end of the house already). Again, there were blinking lights in the corners of the roof. This bedroom had an ensuite. Ryan leaned in and, as promised, saw the taped line, about level with the cistern, marking the area above which was in the camera's view. It looked like the same tape as the roll he had around his wrist. The next room, completing the T, was an office. Again, it was stripped clean other than a bare desk with an unplugged computer sitting ornamentally like in an Ikea display suite. Pulling open the empty drawers, and again thinking that the surfer and Adam had possibly beat him in here, he realised May was just standing in the doorway watching him. She would have had to come down this side of the hallway first, in order to bust him searching the closet. She might have already been in this room too . . . She would have had to be quick, but it wasn't impossible that she'd found an advantage for herself, just like he had.

Back in the corridor, they tried the last door, opposite the entranceway, but it was locked. There wasn't enough room behind the kitchen for another full room, so Ryan assumed, as he had when he'd walked past it originally, that it must lead to a flight of stairs. *But can a clifftop mansion even technically have a basement?* he thought, absent-mindedly.

Ryan gave May an apologetic, *sorry, locked*, grimace and said, 'That's it, I guess. Let's go see what the others are doing.'

'This place is worth more millions than it has bedrooms.' May whistled through her teeth. 'Eat the fuckin' rich, I say.'

TEN

'I'm going to take the money.'

Ryan was hunkered at the corner of the boardroom table with May, where they could both sit comfortably in chairs, each of their hands resting on adjoining corner walls. The clock had just passed the five-hour mark, the dull winter sun bathing the space in orange light. The glass frontage had cooled, and, cold-handed, most contestants had slowly changed positions away from the windows, filtering through the rest of the house. Michelle, prepared with her glove, didn't seem to mind, and sat comfortably on the plush carpet, meditating her way through the boredom. Adam had taken up a kitchen stool and started to complain he was hungry, waving his spare hand at the cameras every fifteen minutes or so, and then grumbling words like *torture* and *prison*. The surfer kept ambling around the place, deliberately getting in people's personal space and not talking to anyone. Maybe he was hoping someone would take their hand off the wall to sock him one if he riled everyone up enough. Lisa and Ned were at the other end of the house, no doubt poking around. Everyone, except meditating Michelle, had made the trip down the hall to explore at some point in the afternoon.

'What?' May was right to be surprised; Ryan had surprised himself with his decision. He'd been thinking about it, but he hadn't really been sure until the words came out of his mouth. He was going to take the money. Maybe he said it out loud to commit to it. Maybe he wanted her to talk him out of it. Either way, it slid out. May realised others might hear and lowered her voice. 'If I had both hands available, I'd shake you. Why the hell would you do that? We've only been here five hours.'

'It's a lot of money.'

'Four million dollars is a lot more.'

Ryan sighed. 'Yes, the house is amazing, but that money is guaranteed if I take it now. It's the sensible choice. This whole thing, it feels *too easy*. It feels wrong.' *No tickets*, he told himself. In his mind he was standing on the street at dawn in the neon light sign of the VIP lounge. If he wasn't the first to go, if someone quit ahead of him and took the money, he didn't want to gamble his daughter's future on a one in six chance.

'Too easy?' May said. 'The kids running this – because that's all they are, kids – are richer than you or I could ever be, just because they upload silly videos. Michelle said they gave away an Aston Martin. Brayden's beanie is Gucci. Some people make a living playing video games. Sometimes opportunity falls in your lap. You've got to grab it with both hands.' May looked at the wall and smiled. 'Well, one hand, in this case.'

Ryan shook his head. 'I believe you get what you deserve, and you deserve what you get.'

May tapped her tongue on her teeth in a tut. 'That's a pretty jaded philosophy of life, Ryan. I hope that's not what you tell your daughter.'

He didn't think she meant it to be cutting, but, in a way she couldn't have known, it was. He realised, from her casual mention of Lydia, that he'd been talking to May the same way he talked to his daughter. What had the performer said to him? *You tell her Santa isn't real, too?* Was he pressing his dour, beaten-down view of life on his daughter? Yes, he'd had a rough few years. But was he displacing all of his hurt, all of his grief since his wife's death, onto Lydia?

'Okay. Say I agree with you there. I *am* being soft.'

'Agreed.'

'That money would still change my life. My daughter's life.'

'Well, my first argument is that you don't want to leave me in here with these *weirdos*. But, seriously, you said your daughter applied for you, right?'

Ryan nodded.

'Well, what's she going to think when you're the first one out? On the *first* night? Isn't she going to be watching? The money's not going anywhere for now – no one else seems to have their eye on it. See how you feel in the next few hours. Think about her and your wife, cheering you on, rooting for you.'

'I've had some . . . trouble. I can't . . .' He lowered his head, aware that the cameras were watching, that they probably had microphones, and what he was about to confess would be heard by the world. 'I can't gamble with my daughter's future. I've done that before.'

May's expression softened and she glanced back at the bag.

'I made some bad decisions after my wife passed away,' Ryan continued, 'and . . .'

'Oh, God. I'm sorry. I thought, when you said you had a family . . .'

'I said I had a daughter. Michelle said I had a family.'

'And you're wearing a ring . . .'

'I do it to remember her. It's okay.'

'No, it's not.' She laughed then, soft and warm. 'I don't know why I'm even trying to talk you into staying; it's easier for me if there's one less of us.'

'Or you're trying to keep the money in play for yourself,' Ryan said, only half joking. 'Why are you here? There's got to be more to your story.'

'You're either untrusting or onto me,' May answered, weaving around his question. She reached across with her free hand to squeeze his, then remembered she needed permission. 'May I?' At Ryan's nod, she took his hand. 'You've had a much harder road than I have,' May said. 'Take the money. Change your life.'

Ryan nodded. But he wasn't so sure anymore. May was right about Lydia watching. She *would* be rooting for him. And maybe he needed to show her every now and then that life is not about pulling back the magician's curtain and seeing the dusty backstage, the machinery in the magic box, and that good things do happen sometimes if you go with the flow. Life is a balance between luck and work, and he'd tipped his philosophical balance too far to one side. It wasn't really about the money. It was only about one thing: would Lydia want him to stay? That was the real question.

Still, something was better than nothing. The money would buy him *time*; buy him a few more years, at least, on the hamster wheel, and then maybe things would improve. He'd be foolish not to take it. Lydia would understand. Surely?

'You know,' Ryan said, 'Rita and I, we knew we'd never live somewhere like this. But we'd always joke about it . . . She would have liked the view.' He shook his head shyly. 'I don't know why I'm telling you this.'

'You do what's right for you,' May said.

He made up his mind.

He slowly started to peel his palm from the wall.

A deafening air horn blasted through the house. It was so loud it rattled the windows, prickled their skin.

'Was that you?' May's eyes were wild. 'Did you move?'

'I was about to. I hadn't done it yet.'

Ryan looked at his hand, just to be sure. His palm was lifted but his fingertips were still touching the wall. He'd stopped, unable to make up his mind, still thinking of his daughter watching him quit.

'What the hell is happening?' Adam shouted.

The surfer smiled.

Michelle spoke calmly, eyes still closed, from her spot on the floor. 'Someone's just been eliminated.'

6 CONTESTANTS REMAINING

ELEVEN

It was Ned, skulking off down the driveway in the dusk, shoulders hunched.

Ryan, May and Adam had hurried to the front door, where they'd bumped into Lisa, already there, watching through the open entrance.

'What happened?' May asked.

'I don't know.' Lisa shrugged. 'We were looking through the rooms, I turned around to go through the drawers and that was when the horn blasted. He must have slipped.'

'Far out. Quick as that, hey?' Adam said. 'Good warning for the rest of us.'

'He looks pissed,' Ryan said, pointing at Ned's walk of shame. Ned's shoulders weren't hunched in disappointment, they were coiled and tense, accompanying his gruff, angry strides. He was shaking his head vehemently.

The three CashSmashers rushed through the gate, cameras swinging from their wrists, now with blinding white lights affixed to the top. They whipped around Ned like fireflies, one of them shouting questions Ryan couldn't quite hear. Brayden put his hand on Ned's shoulder to slow him down.

That was when Ned whirled, grabbed Brayden by the collar, and pushed him up to the edge of the fountain. Brayden went pale, squirming under the big man's frame, the balls of his feet pedalling on the lip of the fountain. His friends didn't help, just kept filming, no doubt salivating at the views this confrontation would bring.

Ned's next words came out as a low, threatening growl. Ryan only caught half of it, and even then he wasn't sure he'd heard it correctly. 'I'm leaving . . . Touch me again . . . If you even think about . . . footage . . . I'll fucking kill you.'

Then Ned gave Brayden a little shove and let go of his collar. Unbalanced, and with thin footing on the slippery ledge, Brayden wobbled for a second and then fell backwards, landing with a splash, arse-first in the fountain. He shook his head, held up a sodden camera, the light on top on the fritz, watching water dribble out of it. He said something snappy to Lucas, who turned and followed Ned out to the street, filming him as he left but making sure to keep his distance. Then Brayden saw the rest of them watching, huddled around the doorway. He thwacked his hand down in the water, sending up a spray, and yelled, like a petulant child, 'What are you all looking at?'

TWELVE

Pizza, as a one-handed food, was probably the CashSmashers' first well-thought-out decision of the day. They hadn't thought through the garlic bread quite so well, though; it had come in a big loaf and Lucas, despite searching through the drawers, hadn't found any cutlery to chop it with, so he'd just left it on the bench, where it remained. The knife block must have been a prop, Ryan figured, as Lucas didn't go for them. That made sense: it would be pretty crazy to put real knives in a house full of people you were trying to drive insane.

The food had arrived about an hour after Ned left, leaving Ryan wondering if they'd delayed ordering food to see if hunger played a part in the first elimination. People get irrational when they're hungry, inattentive. Maybe it had worked. Although Ryan judged that the anger on Ned's face as he left was more than just hunger.

There had been a sort of unspoken territory division established in the main room. Adam had staked his claim on the kitchen. May and Ryan had returned to their corner of the table; the bisecting walls were a handy place to maintain their touch securely, and the chairs were comfortable. Michelle was calmly sitting where she'd started, clearly thinking that moving too much was the way to fail. The surfer was still floating around, irritating people. Lisa didn't have a spot in the main room but had taken up camp in one of the bedrooms, and so perhaps she was willing to risk a doze. When the pizzas arrived, Lisa emerged and decided to hand them around. She couldn't be bothered walking over to the surfer and frisbeed a box to him. He raised a slice, toppings lost in the throw, in a sarcastic 'cheers'.

Even the meal had a strategy to it. Ryan was hungry, but he didn't want to stuff himself so full that he'd feel lethargic, and it had occurred to him that it might pay to manage bowel movements too. He'd scoffed one piece before he realised this, and then nibbled a second piece slowly.

The bag of money still sat in the centre of the room. Through all the commotion of Ned's departure, and then the arrival of the food, Ryan's thoughts of taking it had been put on the backburner. He'd now ticked off seven and a half hours. It was black outside, the glittering stars and a few glowing lights of ships on the ocean not enough to light the room, the soft glow of the fireplace turning the white carpet orange. He'd already lasted longer than he thought he might. And he was one of six now. The odds still didn't win him over, but he'd be lying if he didn't think he was an inch closer to the prize. The *ticket*. Maybe there was a bit more of his old self in him now, weighing up the odds. But more important was the thought that May had reminded him of: Lydia was watching. Maybe with her friends. Pointing at the screen and saying *that's my dad*. He could stay a little longer, for sure.

'Why didn't Ned take the money?' Ryan thought aloud.

'Probably against the rules,' May suggested. 'Maybe you have to *choose* to go for the money when you leave. If he just slipped, why should he be rewarded? Maybe that's why he was so pissed off when he left: they told him he couldn't go back and get the cash.'

It was a good theory. Perhaps you had to get the money before the air horn sounded. It made sense: the money was supposed to be a choice, not a compensation. 'He seemed in a hurry to get out of here.'

'Wouldn't you be? Why stay? He looks like he plays sports, right? So he's probably competitive. He'd just be furious that he was first. He must have felt he wasted his time.'

'Anyone want a slice of ham and pineapple?' Ryan called to the room, aware that they probably all had different-flavoured pizzas. No one said anything, so he added sarcastically, 'Good chat. It's going to be a long night in silence.'

'What do you want to talk about, man?' Adam piped up. He'd started nibbling on the loaf of garlic bread, peeling the foil down and chewing the top, without, Ryan noted, having asked the others if they wanted a bite.

'Dunno. I Spy?'

Surprisingly, the suggestion elicited an enthusiastic response, with even the surfer roped into playing (his snide answer to *I spy with my little eye something beginning with R* had been *runners-up*). After the food and surviving the first elimination, there was, briefly, a sense of communal feeling in the group. But of course it was only temporary. The game eventually dissolved around ten-thirty, when an argument kicked off around Adam insisting that 'moonlight' was two words, beginning with M and L.

Now it was getting late, the next challenge presented itself: sleep. Whether to risk it or push through. Adam looked the drowsiest, but he was keeping himself awake, cricking his neck. Michelle seemed the most comfortable, her hand still on the metal feature wall that joined the curved glass, her back to the window, leaning against her outstretched arm. She looked like she might risk sleeping in that position, but if she slipped forwards she'd be done for. Ryan guessed she had about a twenty-five per cent chance of slipping. The surfer had chosen to lie on his back on the carpet, arm out to his side and his eyes shut, but he was definitely awake. A much riskier position if he nodded off: Ryan gave it odds of fifty-fifty. No one was chancing the other rooms. Lisa had disappeared down there for a bit, but just when Ryan thought she might be taking a nap, she'd come back with a stripped bedsheet. She'd knotted it into a prison-style escape rope and fashioned it into a lasso, and then spent an hour trying to toss it one-handed over the bag of cash. She was trying to win the money without quitting. It was a good thing she was such a terrible shot and the bag was heavy, so she couldn't get any purchase. Ryan watched carefully. If she did get it moving, he decided he'd sprint for it.

He still entertained the idea of leaving at any time, even as he tried to figure out how to sleep. He stood up, pushed his chair to the side and lowered himself to the floor. Legs out, back to the wall, seemed to be the best position. Though it still had its risks: if he leaned to the side it lowered the chance of him tilting one way or another, which was clearly Michelle's strategy. But it was too risky if he fell forward, or his arm went limp. He was going to have to just push through without sleep.

That was when he remembered the duct tape. *Jackpot!*

He slid it off his wrist, levered a fingernail under the join and used his teeth to rip a fluttering strip off. He lined up his hand with a comfortable spot on the wall, not too high and not too low, and pasted the tape over it. He did this six or seven more times until a robust star of tape secured him to the wall. It looked like Spider-Man had shot webs at him. He smiled, pleased with his ingenuity. It wouldn't do permanently – he would have to redo it every time he went to the bathroom, for example, and he would run out of tape after a few of those – but it was good enough to allow him to sleep now. He gave it a couple of jolts to be sure. His tape-glove held well. Almost too well, he thought, hoping the place didn't catch fire.

'You can't do that,' Michelle said.

Ryan looked over. She had her eyes open, squinting.

'Hey!' She waved at the cameras in the roof. 'Can you see this? He can't do that, it's cheating!'

So much for an alliance.

'I didn't bring it with me. I found it here. It's part of the game.' Though he felt stupid addressing the invisible jury, Ryan also found himself talking to the roof, hoping the cameras could hear him. 'I can use what I found in the house, right?'

'It's unfair,' Michelle moaned.

'It's not an advantage, it's a reward,' May said, defending him. 'He found it. *You* haven't moved. No wonder you don't have anything like it.'

'Yeah, man, I don't think it's right,' Adam meekly contributed, taking Michelle's side.

Lisa didn't speak. But she wore a barely concealed scowl, clearly annoyed that Ryan had an advantage, but she couldn't say so or she'd look like a hypocrite after her use of the bedsheet to try to hook the bag.

'It should be against the rules!' Michelle said, still waving an arm. 'Are you even watching this thing?'

A crackling of static came from the roof, and Ryan now saw the speaker that had blared the air horn. It was affixed to the central chimney column of the fireplace. One of the boys' voices came through. They were indistinguishable, but Ryan assumed it was the ringleader, Brayden.

'Objects in the house can be used.'

There was a click as the speaker disconnected. If it wouldn't have got her eliminated, Michelle would no doubt have thrown both her hands up in frustration. She glared at Ryan, seething. Lisa didn't seem to react to the decision. May looked impressed. Adam started wrenching open all the kitchen drawers, clicking his tongue with disappointment at their emptiness. The only items not bolted down were two ice trays in the freezer and the knife block, and that would only be useful if it was real and he planned on murdering all the other contestants. It occurred to Ryan, though, watching Adam pillage the kitchen, that the knife block itself, if he tipped the knives out, might be heavy enough to make a grapple out of the bedsheet rope. He filed the thought away for later.

Ryan noticed the surfer was staring at him. Frustrated, Ryan surprised himself by lashing out. 'You got a problem with this as well, I suppose?'

'Fine by me.' The surfer shook his head, pointing to Ryan's hand, taped to the wall. 'But once I own this place, you'll be popping around to fix the paint job.'

THIRTEEN

Ryan woke up three times in the night.

The first time: there was a clunk at the table above him. He opened his eyes to see May slapping her cheeks with her free hand. She must have almost slipped into sleep and was desperately trying to make sure it didn't happen again. Ryan looked around the room. The others were dark lumps of shadow in the flickering light of the now-dying fire; a few glints of eyes, like wolves in a forest, showed a couple were awake. Others he wasn't sure about. There was no air horn yet, though. He was pretty sure Lisa's shadow wasn't where it had been earlier. She seemed to have staked out the bedroom end of the house as her own. He thought Adam was still in the kitchen. Michelle hadn't moved. The surfer was against the far window, a black smudge on the moonlit ocean.

The digital timer glowed red. Eleven hours and forty-two minutes. Ryan didn't wear a watch and his phone was in the lock box. He'd arrived at midday, and spent some time waiting for everyone, going through introductions and having the rules explained, meaning they'd started about half past twelve. That meant it was after midnight. Ryan's shoulder ached from not moving; he flexed the joint but it didn't help much. He remembered Michelle saying her last competition had lasted seventy-two hours. A memory of her in that video, her walking off despondent, arm cradled like a limp snake, flashed through his mind. There was a long way to go.

Another bang from the table. May's head had dropped and shot back up again. She could barely keep her eyes open. She clearly wouldn't make it through the night.

'Hey,' he whispered. 'You okay?'

May gave him a defeated smile and a sad nod. He could see she didn't want to give up, but she was done – too proud or too tired to take the money until the very last minute. But by then, she might have missed her chance.

He took a gamble. 'Listen, you're not here for yourself, are you? There's a look people get when they want to win something for themselves. You don't have that look.'

May put her spare hand on his shoulder and squeezed it. 'You know what it's like to fight for someone else, don't you?' she said. Then, in a tone that was more empathy than sympathy, she said, 'Your wife, was she sick?'

Ryan nodded, understanding what she was really trying to share with him. 'Yes. And you? Is it someone you love?'

May looked like she was about to say more, but then her eyes flicked up to the nearest camera in the roof and she held her tongue. 'I'm going to keep going for a little while,' she said, then yawned. They both knew she was lying. 'Tell me if anyone goes for the bag of money, will you? I'm just going to shut my eyes for a second.'

She closed her eyes and laid her head against the wall. She stayed like that for a while, and then her grip on his hand started to loosen. It would only be seconds before she went completely slack and her other hand slipped from the wall.

Ryan shook her back to consciousness. 'Here.' He held out the duct tape.

May's eyes widened like a child who'd just unwrapped a toy they'd begged for at Christmas. She didn't even bother to decline under the pretence of polite haggling, snatching it hungrily and pulling two lengthy strips of tape off with her teeth – Ryan's stomach lurching at the amount she used, like it did when you gave someone a bite of something and thought, *well, go easy* – and pasting them over her hand in a wide X.

She handed him back the tape, gave a sigh of relief and mouthed *thank you*.

The second time: he was only half awake, roused by a long, drawn-out, scraping sound. It was the sound from a million slasher films, when the killer is dragging an axe by the handle, its head bumping against the concrete. The scraping sound wasn't enough to wake him fully – he didn't even open his eyes to check the clock – it was just a muffled presence, half inside a dream and half inside reality.

The third time: it was the motion sensor that woke him up. It clicked on a light over the deck, shining brightly into the living room through the glass panorama. Ryan winced, groggily went to cover his eyes, and felt a resistive tug in his shoulder. Stuck. He remembered where he was. *Shit.* He was glad he'd taped himself to the wall, otherwise he'd have just been eliminated. It was that simple to slip up. The light hadn't woken May yet. She was above him, still sitting in a chair, her head slumped on the table. Her shoulder was folded back, arm stretched out behind her where she'd fastened it, bent like someone was trying to make her tap out in a wrestling match.

Though the light had come on, nothing moved outside. Mist shrouded the surface of the heated pool. A sequence of underwater LEDs had also flicked on, making the water glow a soft yellow.

The wind, lashing the house as it whipped across the clifftop, made the glass panels creak. The red clock said fourteen and a half hours. The outdoor sensor light clicked off. Must have been an animal, Ryan thought, as he laid his head back against the wall.

A high-pitched scream cut through the night.

It was shrill, terrified, definitely a woman, and gone almost as soon as it started. It had seemed to come from outside, he thought, but the motion sensor light hadn't flicked back on, so he couldn't see anything in the dull moonlight across the deck. The low glow of the fire inside allowed him to see a few of the clumped shadows dotted around the room starting to move. He listened for another scream, but there was only the rustle of people waking up.

Then the poolside light clicked back on. Ryan saw it immediately.

On one of the panes of glass, a smeared, bloody handprint.

FOURTEEN

Ryan was still processing it when a woman he didn't recognise stumbled across the deck, clutching at her stomach with one hand. She was wearing a formal dress, some kind of silky fabric in emerald green, though it was a dark black around her mid-section. There was a bubbling ooze coming from between the fingers on the hand she had clamped to her side. She looked behind her and gave another scream, and then she spotted all of them inside and ran to the window, pounding on the glass again, before her energy ran out and she collapsed to the ground, her hand sliding down the glass, leaving a crimson streak. She stayed motionless, a sprawled figure at the base of the window.

Ryan made to stand, forgetting about the duct tape, which wrenched his fixed hand back, making him fall back to a sitting position. He swore and started quickly picking at the corners. He'd used enough tape to give him a secure sleep, but that meant he was well and truly stuck.

May raised her head. 'What's happening?' she murmured, groggy. Had she really slept through all that?

'Someone's hurt,' Ryan said, trying to get his nail under the tape. 'Hey! Wake up! Everyone wake up! Someone help her!'

He looked around the room. Adam was still in the kitchen, shaking. It looked like he hadn't slept at all and had seen exactly what Ryan had. May yawned, still waking up, not understanding the seriousness just yet. Hadn't she heard the scream?

Michelle was looking at Ryan without sympathy. 'You help her,' she said bluntly. She was still pissed off that Ryan had found the tape, he realised.

'I'm trying. I'm stuck to the *fucking* wall.' He wrenched the tape harder, as it started to give. 'You seriously care about this stupid game anymore?'

Michelle shrugged.

The surfer stood up. He was jigging up and down on the spot, agitated. Ryan noticed Lisa wasn't in the room. Had he got a good enough look at the injured woman to know it wasn't her? She hadn't *sounded* like Lisa, both in terms of her voice and the lack of jangling jewellery, but he wasn't sure. He got a strip of tape off, clumps of paint and tiny chunks of plaster coming with it. He could feel his palm lifting, but not enough.

'Hey, kid!' the surfer shouted. 'You've got an oath, right? Help the goddamn woman.'

Adam shook his head, refusing to make eye contact. 'I'm a student. I haven't taken the oath yet.'

'Well, you know how to fucking help her, so help her.'

'Don't look at me.' Adam looked at the floor.

Then there was a low, long groan. The woman had started to crawl towards the edge of the swimming pool. She hauled herself on her elbows, limp legs dragging a bloody trail. Under her moans was a slow buzzing, ominous and out of place in the night. More danger?

The surfer was now jumping out of his skin, looking around the room. Weighing up his options. He appealed to them. 'I don't know first aid, guys. The kid should go.'

'Come and make me.' It was surprisingly assertive from Adam.

'No one could possibly be so . . .' Ryan was about to call them heartless – he couldn't believe they were all still *playing* – when he realised something else. No one *would* let another person die for four million dollars. Unless . . .

'What's going on?' May asked again, still struggling to open her eyes. 'Why's everyone shouting?'

'Can't you see her? Jesus, wake up.' Ryan waved at the camera in the roof. 'Hey! Lucas? Brayden? Anyone? Can you see this? Is no one going to help her?'

'Oh, fuck this. Fuck all of you,' the surfer said, shaking his head, banging his spare fist against the glass and finally hissing, 'Fine!'

Then he let go of the wall. He sprinted across the centre of the room, wrenching open the kitchen door and running to the woman. He crouched down and rolled her over, searching for a pulse on her neck. The woman's eyes were wide. She reached up a bloodied hand, smearing red across the surfer's cheek. Then she started violently convulsing, her back arching, shoulders bucking.

Then the buzzing got louder. That was when Ryan realised that something was wrong. The surfer did too. He stood, taking a step back from the woman's writhing body. He reached up and touched his bloody cheek, shaking his head as a look of horror dawned across his face.

The woman wasn't convulsing. She was . . . laughing.

An air horn blared.

5 CONTESTANTS
REMAINING

FIFTEEN

The fireflies of the hand-held lights and cameras appeared in a rush, tracing glowing trails in the air as they weaved around in the dark, enclosing the surfer, wild-eyed and speechless, in their glare. He looked down in shock at the woman on the ground, then marvelled at his blood-red hands as if he'd just discovered them.

Ryan realised the ominous buzz in the background was the whir of the drone – filming the whole thing from above. He'd pieced it together just before he'd got his own hand off the wall. He'd been watching Adam's and Michelle's refusal to help, feeling sickened, before he'd had the sudden realisation. Adam was the youngest there; he'd have seen plenty of the CashSmashers' videos, and Michelle had played before. They hadn't believed it was real from the get-go.

Consciousness returned to the surfer's eyes. He clenched his jaw, neck bulging, then turned and wrenched open the door that led into the kitchen. The YouTubers scurried in after him, spreading across the room. The surfer lasered in on Adam immediately, storming over to him, nose to nose, puffing out his chest. Adam tried to keep his back straight but couldn't help cowering slightly.

Lisa finally emerged from the corridor, bleary-eyed, but took in enough of the scene to know she shouldn't say anything.

'Did you know it was fake?' the surfer growled.

Adam didn't say anything. His Adam's apple did a bungee jump as he swallowed hard.

'*She* knew. She's played before.' The surfer pointed at Michelle. 'But *you* . . .' He shook his head. 'I'm trying to decide if you did too, or if you were willing to watch someone else *in pain* just so you could line your own pockets. Just to win this stupid thing.' He spat each word. 'Did. You. Know?' Then he smiled, his grin turning into a slow accepting nod. He'd decided he already knew the answer. He seemed surprisingly calm as he turned away from Adam to leave.

But then he whipped back around, an explosion of movement, and slammed his fist into the kitchen cabinet, right above Adam's head.

Adam flinched . . . but his hand didn't leave the wall.

The surfer laughed. 'All right. I guess that's it, then.' He clicked his tongue. 'Can I take the money?'

Lucas and Brayden shook their heads.

The surfer walked across the room. When he passed May, he leaned over and mimicked her in a high-pitched whine, 'Why's everyone screaming?' Then in his normal voice, to Ryan, 'Don't buy it. You tried, at least.'

Lucas followed him down the corridor and Ryan heard the front door open. Brayden stayed to do an interview with the bloodied woman. She looked much more alive now, tossing her hair back and laughing, throwing up peace signs. Ryan figured she was another YouTuber, a friend of theirs. Behind her, dawn was starting to colour the horizon, a peachy haze on the edge of the sea.

Ryan had made a mess of his tape-fastening, but it would be too risky to go back to sleep without redoing it, and he didn't want to use any extra tape as he'd need it for the next night. But that wasn't too much of a problem. Ryan couldn't have slept if he'd wanted to.

The surfer's voice echoed through the house, one last bitter taunt. 'Erosion's a bitch. I hope whoever wins slides into the sea.'

SIXTEEN

Ryan grew to hate the timer as it ticked onwards with the maniacal slowness of a classroom clock. Any brief camaraderie the group had developed had dissolved after the mid-dawn elimination, with everyone more aware of their fragile position and the slowly increasing odds. So they each kept to their stations, concentrating less on conversation or even argument, and instead focusing solely on their hand on the wall. Breakfast was delivered: muffins and sports drinks. Adam tossed Ryan a bottle that was near impossible to catch, hoping he'd move off the wall to grab it. Ryan watched the bottle sail past, rolling into the middle of the room. Adam shrugged, as if to say *worth a shot*, and threw him another.

The clock clicked over to twenty-four hours without further incident.

The midday sunlight dazzled through the glass frontage. There was a scar of translucent red in the middle of the plush white carpet, cast by the bloody handprint on the window as if it were stained glass.

Ryan assessed his competition. Michelle seemed the most comfortable, well rested, propped in her corner, eyes shut in a meditative state unless something started happening. She hadn't been to the bathroom yet. Ryan figured that her strategy was not to let anyone else see her move. She wanted to appear threatening, like she was doing the best, and so perhaps she'd gone secretly in the night. Or she'd just sat in it – Ryan wouldn't put it past her. She hadn't even flinched at the screaming woman; she knew enough about the CashSmashers' gimmicks and the stunts they'd try to pull. So did Adam, Lisa and possibly May. Ryan, having watched a couple of their videos and heard the stories from Lydia, should have anticipated such tricks as well, but he'd been sucked into the emotion of the moment. They were all tired and mentally stretched, and it had looked real enough to him. What had Adam said about the TV show that tried to stop people from sleeping? *People went literally psychotic . . .*

Lisa showed up for meals but was otherwise down the hall. That was another good strategy; she'd missed the early morning drama and by the time she'd got to the main room, it had resolved itself. She was also, perhaps, avoiding the glaring eyes of the other contestants, hoping, maybe, that minor slips might go unnoticed by the smaller number of cameras in the bedrooms. But Ryan thought it was equally dangerous: being on her own made her more susceptible to sleep or lapses in concentration. Adam had slept the least and looked haggard, but not despairing; Ryan assumed that med students, with their gruelling schedules, probably had quite good stamina. Though Adam was getting crabbier: he'd snapped at Lucas when the breakfast had been delivered: *would it kill you to give us some coffee?* Out of all of them, Adam was the one looking most frequently at the bag of money.

May had also had a troubled rest of the night: when she didn't have one elbow on the table propping her head up, she was the most mobile, taking hourly walks around the circle. Ryan thought it risky to be moving so much.

He tried to weigh himself up against the others, to think about where he was ranking. His shoulders were starting to seize, so he rolled his neck, but he'd had more sleep than some. He'd been to the bathroom that morning, so he'd be okay for a while before he had to move again. The roll of tape on his wrist was a comfort: his biggest advantage. But despite all that, he had some serious issues that might lengthen his odds. If he hadn't been taped up, he would have fallen for the bloodied woman last night for sure, so he was easy to trick. And he desperately needed the bag of money. Not to mention it had now been a full day away from his daughter. He missed her.

He wondered if this was live, if she was watching, or if she was forcing her grandmother to figure out the complexities of YouTube and watching all the CashSmashers' previous videos in preparation. Ryan had watched Lydia and Rita yelling at some television show as a contestant made a boneheaded decision to quit. It always seemed so simple, so cowardly, from home. But he understood it now. On screen, it always looked like the contestant was walking away from the prize. But thinking about his daughter, Ryan realised that the answer to that question – would he throw away the chance of getting four million dollars to see his daughter? – was yes. Without hesitation. So his flaw was that he wasn't focused. He had plenty of reasons to leave. He didn't have his head in the game enough. All things considered, he put himself somewhere in the middle of the pack.

'You all right?' May was looking at him. His thoughts must have been printed on his face.

'Yeah. You?'

'Never better. That bag's looking pretty good right now, isn't it?'

Ryan rolled his tongue around his teeth in thought. 'It is.'

'I was thinking, you said you were in trouble. Before.'

'Did I?' Ryan shrugged it off.

She thought for a second. 'Look, don't get upset if I'm off the mark, but the way you said it got me thinking. This is going online to millions of viewers. If you owe people money, don't you think *they'll* be watching this? They might want you to . . . you know.'

That hit Ryan in the gut. He hadn't thought of that. Would his dodgy loan sharks be expecting him to take the money? Would they be mad if he didn't? May had made a scarily good point.

'She wants you to take it,' Michelle murmured from across the room. 'It improves her chances. And think about it: who are you going to give the tape to when you leave?'

Ryan paused to consider. Here was a woman he'd only met yesterday asking him to take the money, as if she knew him. He managed a small laugh but couldn't look May in the eye. 'Yesterday you talked me into staying and now you're trying to talk me into leaving.'

'I was just making conversation,' May said, lifting her voice to get across the room to Michelle. 'She's the one with the mind games.'

'She's just needling us,' Ryan said. Michelle put her head back against the window, a smug smile creeping across her face. Ryan *knew* Michelle was playing with them. But it didn't mean she wasn't right. How hard was May playing? The surfer had mocked her when he left: *why's everyone screaming?* Did it really take that long to wake up? Did she not realise what was happening, or did she not care? Ryan remembered the surfer's growl at Adam, and maybe the same question applied to May: *Did you know?*

And why was she talking about his *trouble*? He'd told her something yesterday, but only obliquely. What was she asking him to do, really? And who was she asking him for? Or was she just reaching into his psyche – she was a psychologist, after all – in an attempt to manipulate him into doing what she wanted: to stay or leave when it suited her?

Or was this whole thing just making him paranoid? His thoughts were becoming irrational. *Literally psychotic.*

But hang on, he chastised himself, that wasn't entirely fair. He'd been generous in giving her his tape so she could sleep through the night but, if he was really honest with himself, hadn't that been more selfishness than chivalry? She knew she was about to lose, and he was worried she would go for the money. He wanted to keep her there so the money remained in play. That was his back-up plan. Sure, May was playing. But, it turned out, so was he.

At twenty-seven hours, Lisa emerged for some exercise, walking laps of the lounge for half an hour. She'd politely excuse herself past the women, stepping over Michelle and arching her body around May, but press herself against Adam and Ryan, as if walking around them was much more difficult. Flirting was a strategy, Ryan supposed, unmoved. Though Adam blushed each time she passed with a sweet *excuse me, sorry, just one second, whoops, sorry, bit close there!* On one lap, as she crossed Michelle, she swore and dropped to her knees, patting the carpet with one hand, armpit in Michelle's face.

'Damn it,' she tsked. 'There's literally nowhere it could have gone.' She patted near Michelle's hips. 'Sorry, love. I dropped an earring. It must be here somewhere. Would you mind shifting?'

'Maybe it rolled over there.' Michelle pointed back up the corridor. Her message was clear: *get lost.* 'Don't you have enough, anyway?'

Lisa rolled her eyes. She spent another minute searching the carpet. Ryan couldn't tell if it was a strategy to get Michelle to move, or if Lisa had genuinely lost an earring, but she was frustrated either way. She stood up and spat, 'When you get booted, I'll come back and get it.'

Half an hour later, the patio door slammed with such ferocity that some of them almost leapt off the wall. Adam, closest to it in the kitchen, held his wrist for the next twenty minutes or so, eyes wide with apprehension, then decided he no longer liked his position in the kitchen, walking over to the side of the pit and sitting there instead.

At thirty hours, Lucas came into the house, delivering, to Adam's delight, coffee and sandwiches. He had a backpack on, from which he pulled some firewood and used it to reinvigorate the embers in the pit. Then he walked over to the black bag, unzipped it and pulled two plastic-wrapped cubes of money out of his backpack, which he slid into the black bag. He made no mention of the value, but they were large green bricks. They all watched him do it, even Lisa, who had come out for the food. Then, without a word, he left.

Two bricks of hundred-dollar notes looked like a fair amount of cash to Ryan. Maybe the bag was now enough to turn it all around. The scales were tipping. He'd outlasted two eliminations; that was enough for his pride and to live up to his daughter's cheerleading. Surely now with the added money there was enough in there that he'd be stupid not to take it.

'Your arm's tense, ready to move,' May said. It surprised him that she was watching him; then again, maybe not. 'Take it if you want,' she added.

He was about to, when Adam said from across the room, 'How do you know it's real?'

'What do you mean?'

'They faked that bloodied woman. What else in here is fake? How do you know the money's real?'

That gave Ryan pause. He hadn't thought of that. Maybe the cash was a trick, designed to embarrass whoever was greedy enough to go for it. He thought about the other videos he'd watched: the woman with her broken-down car, on her last dollar, with fifty grand floating down to her. He'd thought at the time it was *too* perfect. 'I watched that money over Chicago video,' he said. 'Was that faked?'

'Looked real to me,' May said. 'Just my opinion, though.'

'That lawyer was real,' Lisa interrupted. Then, reading the look of confusion on Ryan's face, she continued. 'You know? The guy in the suit who was pushed into the river. He hit his head on a rock, has a permanent brain injury. He could have died. I think they settled with him out of court, but it was pretty full-on for a while. They didn't script that, I guarantee it.'

'You think it's real, then? The money.'

'I think sometimes they're playing tricks on us, and other times they're letting us play tricks on ourselves. This game's in your head more than it is in your hand.' She tapped her forehead with her free hand.

It was by no means conclusive, but it was enough to keep Ryan by the wall. The conversation dried up and they were back to their wary, adversarial silence.

As the sun set for the second time, the bag of money remained untouched. The slash of red light on the carpet pointed to it like an arrow.

SEVENTEEN

The long, slow axe-scraping sound woke Ryan again.

He'd been dreaming of his wife, in the way that he often did, a vision manifested from grief and memory, that almost felt real when her dream-self wrapped her arms around his shoulder from behind and she nibbled on his ear. He liked those dreams, and he tried to hang on to them. In this one, they were sitting on the beach, looking up at the houses on the clifftops, pointing at the ones they knew were far too expensive for them to even stay a night in, and saying: *I'll live there one day.* She was holding his hand. They laughed as he wrinkled his nose disdainfully at the four-storey mansion and said, *I guess we could renovate.* This was a good dream. He could feel her hand in his. Then it was gone.

His nose was cold, so it must have been early. This time, not wanting to give the timer the psychological victory of revealing how little time had really passed, he kept his eyes squeezed shut. He heard the distant hiss of waves charging the cliffs below. There was a faint whispering from the corridor, consisting of tense, bitten-off words. Next to him, May's soft breathing. He'd given her the tape again so she could sleep, though this time he'd personally rationed out the length of her strips. He figured he had enough for himself for two more nights, or both of them for one, which was a choice he wasn't looking forward to making. Partly because if it got down to the two of them, he'd have to outlast her, and he wasn't sure he could. And partly because he felt horrible at the prospect of letting May down. She'd told him she was playing for someone else too, implying they were sick, just like Rita had been. He could hardly rob her of that chance. Unless, the thought flickered, that was how she *wanted* him to feel. She was a psychologist after all.

There were no more screams that night. What happened next happened in silence.

4 CONTESTANTS REMAINING

EIGHTEEN

Ryan prised his eyes open, surprised to see daylight, which meant that they'd all made it through another night without the blare of the air horn. May's head was heavy on his shoulder, where she'd accidentally tilted during the night. He smiled, regret flooding through him over yesterday's paranoia about her strategy. But then he spotted Adam, obvious in his doctor's scrubs, on his back in the epicentre of the pit. Asleep.

Ryan's first thought was that Adam had dozed off, perhaps dreaming of quitting and taking the money, and sleep-walked towards it in the night. He was beside the bag of money, one arm stretched out towards it, like a desert traveller who'd expired just before reaching an oasis. Then Ryan thought it was strange the air horn hadn't sounded. And only then did he see the stainless steel of a knife blade glinting in the dawn sunlight, protruding from the young man's stomach.

Ryan shook May awake. She opened her eyes, panicked by his abruptness, and quickly checked her hand, still secured to the wall with an X of tape, before sighing in relief. Then she realised, aghast, that she'd been sleeping on his shoulder. She had a crust of dried saliva on the side of her mouth, which she furtively wiped away.

'Oh, sorry. I must have—'

'It's fine,' Ryan said. He pointed to Adam's body. He spoke without the urgency that seeing a man with a knife in their stomach usually dictates, because nothing in the room felt real. Not the bag with the money in it. Not a possible corpse. 'Look.'

'Is he out?'

'I think he's—'

'What the hell happened to him?' Lisa emerged from the corridor, looking surprisingly well rested. She must have found a good position in one of the bedrooms to help her sleep. Her eyes widened as she took in the shocking tableau.

'Is someone out?' Michelle murmured, without opening her eyes.

Ryan saw something move out on the deck, which might have been nothing, or it could have been a bird, or it could have been a person, flitting past the window. One of the hosts, handheld camera strapped to their palm, sniggering as they ducked out of sight? He wanted to stand up, suddenly feeling trapped in the one spot. He was picking at his overnight fastenings, thinking about how he had to go easy tonight to get as much out of the roll as he could, when he realised that his roll of tape *wasn't* around his wrist anymore. It had disappeared. For some shameful reason, this panicked him more than seeing the knife. That was his lifeline. Gone.

As Ryan processed the loss of his only advantage, Lisa started to panic. 'There's so much blood,' she moaned. She was looking up and down the corridor, where splotches of red on the carpet led back into the hall.

'Oh my God.' May covered her mouth.

Ryan tried to calm everyone. 'Maybe it's . . . I mean . . . Is it for real this time?'

'Of course it's real,' Lisa snapped.

'I think I can smell blood.' May's voice was resigned, mournful.

'When did you . . .?'

'I just woke up,' Ryan defended himself.

'Someone check,' Lisa pleaded.

'You'd like that, wouldn't you?' Michelle smirked. 'I'm not moving.'

'It could be another trick,' May agreed.

'There's a fucking dead body in the middle of the room.' Lisa's pitch was rising. 'Someone do something!'

'I'm not falling for it.' Michelle shook her head, unperturbed.

'Actually, yeah.' May was hesitant, but hopeful. 'Why wasn't there a horn?'

Lisa had started waving at the roof. 'Anybody? Hello? Can you hear us or are you just sitting there and watching, you sick bastards? Anybody? Help! *Help!*'

The speaker crackled. Someone cleared their throat, then there was a pause and the microphone scuffed (Ryan imagined people squabbling, one hand over the receptor: *I know what I'm doing, let me do it*) before a slightly hesitant, belaboured voice came through. Brayden's.

'Keep playing.'

NINETEEN

'You're not seriously going along with this, are you?'

May shrugged. 'You heard them. They want us to keep playing. It's all part of it. How is this any different to last night?'

Michelle had returned to her meditation. Lisa had stormed off down the corridor, swearing at the cameras in the roof.

'*This?*' Ryan pointed to the prone man in the middle of the room. Adam was too far away to check on, which, if it was indeed fake, was a clever move. Ryan would have to quit the game to get close enough to feel for a pulse. 'You think this is the same as last night? It feels so real.'

'Well . . .' May thought for a second, then agreed. 'No . . . They've stepped up their game, obviously. Or maybe we're just more susceptible. We've been here *two days*. You're sleep deprived.'

'I've slept.'

'But you haven't *rested*. If you're anything like me, it's been fitful, your eyes awake under your eyelids. Like sleeping before an alarm you're worried you'll miss. You know the signs of sleep deprivation? Delirium. Hallucinations. Lack of reasoning. All that's enough to make *this*'—she gestured at the body—'seem pretty convincing.'

'He's lying right there, May. I'm not hallucinating.'

'Not yet. But there's paranoia there, in all of us. Be honest. You don't trust me anymore, do you?'

That put an end to his argument. The things he'd thought of her, in his mind, the last two days. She knew. But now she was telling him he couldn't trust himself. And there was a supposed corpse in the middle of the room: could he even trust that?

He changed the topic. 'I heard whispering last night. It sounded tense. Did you hear anything?'

She raised her eyebrows as if to say *now who's hallucinating*? Then she said cautiously, 'I heard some kind of argument from down near the bedrooms.'

'An argument? Were you already awake or was it loud enough to wake you?'

She shook her head at that. 'It's just a game, Ryan.'

'You're talking yourself into thinking this is okay,' Ryan said darkly. Her calmness rattled him, that she would be so accepting. 'This feels wrong.'

'What about this whole thing is normal? Michelle's not leaving the wall – she's in it to the end, even if we all pile up as corpses, and you're not picking on her. And the kids running this are idiots, sure, entitled brats with more money made through less effort than you and I could ever comprehend. But do you really think they wouldn't have called the police by now? They're watching us every second. They would have seen it happen. So, yeah, I *am* justifying it. I've got four million reasons to, okay? You think you're the only one who *needs* to be here.'

'I just—'

'You don't get to tell me what to think when you're still holding on to the wall.'

Ryan looked guiltily at his hand. She was right. For all his bluster, Ryan didn't *quite* believe it either. Whether it was the surrealness of the whole game or the dangling carrot of the house, he wasn't willing to quit for this. The surfer, humiliated as he'd been, had been the only one unselfish enough to make that trade. Now here they were again, four of them left, and none of them would do the same. Silly as the whole game was, the YouTube celebrities in their thousand-dollar beanies had unknowingly constructed a pretty revealing social experiment: this unique torture had exposed his selfishness. May had called his bluff.

And to think, two days ago, he'd wanted to take the cash and walk out. Two days ago, he'd assured himself that he wouldn't buy a ticket. Now not only had the ticket been bought, but he was beginning to think that he stood a chance. He caught himself weighing up his odds, the odds of his competitors, a way of thinking he was sure he'd left behind. Worse still – and the very fact that he was aware of this chilled him – he was beginning to believe he *deserved* to win.

That was how he'd felt at his worst, dawn rising, wallet light. That it was *his* turn. That he was *owed*. No matter how hard he convinced himself he was here for Lydia, he was becoming less sure if this was about what he could win, or if it was just about winning.

There was a downwards slope ahead of him, and he knew the only way to stop sliding was to quit now. Another one of those horrible mental assurances from the throes of his addiction surfaced, the thought that kept him going when he knew he was in deep and getting deeper: *I've come this far.*

'Think about it, okay?' May interrupted his thoughts, her voice soft, her free hand squeezing his shoulder. 'He's young enough to be friends with them. He's even wearing scrubs, so maybe it's a costume. And he's been riling us all up since he got here, right? Who in here hasn't he pissed off? He's got to be one of them. And it makes sense too. The first time they tried to scare us with what's outside the house; now they're trying to make us fear what's inside.

They want us to suspect each other. Hell, maybe we're supposed to solve it. We might get a prize or something.'

'I guess you're right,' Ryan relented. Though he kept staring at Adam, trying to decide if he could see any microscopic lift of the chest, a stray blink or breath. The familiar buzzing started, and Ryan saw the drone drifting back and forth outside of the windowed pit. *They're watching. They want to see what we do. It can't be real.*

May continued. 'And who would be stupid enough to commit a murder *on camera*. This whole place is rigged with them. What would be the point?'

'If it is real'—Ryan gave a weak smile, nodding towards May's taped hand—'at least you and I have pretty solid alibis. We were literally stuck here all night.'

She laughed. 'Sure.'

He almost told her that his tape was gone, that it wouldn't really matter if they quit now or at the end of the day, because he knew there was no way either of them would make it through the night without it. Michelle had her meditation, and Lisa had some other strategy down the bedroom end of the house, which had been working for both of them. Ryan knew he couldn't carry on without slipping. He almost told her, but he didn't, because the tape hadn't just walked off on its own: someone had taken it. It could have been any of them, even the CashSmashers themselves, trying to remove his advantage. He'd become scared of what May could do to him mentally with even the smallest piece of information, so he held it back.

If he was still in it by sunset – if he hadn't lost or, he thought blackly, been murdered by then – he would take the cash. Then he realised that was the third time he'd made this promise to himself, and yet he was still here. He'd made those kind of promises before, standing on a kerb in the early dawn light, listening to the allure of bells and whistles.

'I need to stretch my legs, do you mind?' He stood, straddled May, sliding his hand above hers.

He walked a lap of the house, down the corridor, U-turning at the bedroom doors (all closed; Lisa must have been in one of them) and past the locked door to get back through the kitchen and then around the pit. He was closer to Adam now, and damned if it still didn't look extremely real. But for every question he raised (there was a metallic smell in the air, the type of smell you taste high in the throat, like blood) he had another to rebuff it (how had this all happened without making a sound?). The crackling fire and the drifting smoke masked a lot of the smell anyway. It seemed pretty well set up. The drone still buzzed past the window; the hosts clearly weren't panicked, so why should he be? Ryan gave the drone a lazy wave.

He walked around to Michelle, sliding his arm down the wall to sit next to her. On moving to a crouch, his shoulder suddenly seized and he had to grit his teeth and breathe through the cramp until it faded. Michelle had her head tilted back against the cool glass and seemed, Ryan thought with a twinge of jealousy, very comfortable.

'How's it going, Detective?' she drawled ironically, slanting one eye open.

'I just came to say hi.'

'Did you?'

'Okay, look. If this is some kind of mind-fuck, it's totally working,' he confessed. 'I'm just trying to understand it. You seem to know the most about these guys. Is this on brand?'

'Definitely.' She shrugged. 'This is the YouTube generation: they need high drama, big twists, to make things viral. Their highest-rated video was the fight in Chicago, where the lawyer fell in the river. They would have made millions out of that. More than they settled for, in any case. How much do you think they'll make if we start killing each other?' Her smile was uncomfortably calm. 'What's to understand?'

'I don't know. Have you been sleeping? Or were you awake all night?'

'Are you asking if I saw anything?' She thought for a second, as if weighing up the information's value. Then she shrugged again. 'I told you at the start of this I had a feeling what was coming. To be honest, I thought it would be another car. But I've been practising meditation. I can enter into a sort of . . . trance, I guess. It's a monk thing. There are all these courses you can buy online. Tibetan monks teaching white folks how to *breathe* on Zoom and charging heavily for it. Ha. So much for vows of silence. I came prepared to win a car, sure, but I really came prepared this time. I'm not going to lose again.'

'I heard whispering in the corridor.'

'Yeah, Adam and Lisa were having a bust-up over something,' she said, without hesitation.

'I thought you were in a trance.'

'I said I learned to meditate, not that I learned how to hold in piss for two days. I got up to go to the bathroom.'

'You go in the night so no one sees you move. So that all we see of you is motionless, threatening and invincible. But night-time's when you stretch your legs. Clever.'

'I didn't say that.' She grimaced, annoyed that she'd given away her strategy. 'Anyway, Adam was storming down the corridor as I was coming up it. I'd say he looked mad, but now that I think about it, he looked smug. He knocked into me – which is against the rules, by the way – and almost took me clean off the wall.' She looked at the roof, clearly upset. 'These guys didn't see it, or else they didn't notice or didn't care.'

'You were mad at him, then? You think he should have been eliminated.'

'God, you do think it's real? Was I mad enough to *kill* him?' She straightened her back and glanced towards the camera on the far wall. She knew the collision had been recorded and there was no point lying about it. 'We had words, okay. Was I pissed off? Sure. There are rules to follow. But that was it.' She pointed to a camera that had a field of view directly down the hall. 'They'll have seen it anyway. You think I'd still be here if they saw me stick a knife in him? If you want mad, maybe you should find out what Lisa was yelling at him about.'

'Yelling? That sounds more serious than just a bust-up.'

'I wouldn't have woken up otherwise. There was yelling coming from down there.' She tilted her head towards the corridor. 'You know, with all these questions you're asking me, I'm starting to wonder if *you're* a part of it. Like, maybe it's your job to convince us of all this. You're asking if this is "on brand"? Well, some kind of sabotage, some kind of mole, wouldn't be beyond them either.'

Ryan thought that sounded a bit ridiculous. But then he remembered that he was asking questions instead of walking to the centre of the room and feeling for a pulse, and it didn't seem quite so absurd. Besides, if Adam wasn't really dead, that meant he had to be a plant. In which case, any other one of them could be too.

'Did they do stuff like this to you last time?' he asked.

'Did they try to trick us? Yep, they offered us cash, holidays, lots of little incentives. They set off a fire alarm. Did they knock up a murder to scare us into leaving?' She shook her head. 'No. But that was a hundred-thousand-dollar car, not a four-million-dollar house. They've raised the stakes.'

'So you think it's fake?'

'I am choosing not to have an opinion on anything outside my hand and this wall.'

'Choosing to be ignorant is just as bad as knowing and not doing anything.'

'So you want to know what happened before you go over to help? Sounds like choosing to me. Are we done? You're breaking my Zen.' She closed her eyes.

He didn't finish the full lap, because it would mean stepping over Michelle and he thought that was best avoided, so he traced his way back through the kitchen. He tried to reassure himself that he wasn't the only one who was deciding to stay. In fact, it seemed like he was the only one even considering quitting. Those three boys would be in pretty serious trouble after this, wouldn't they? Surely they had some kind of duty of care to the contestants? Ryan had signed a waiver, but that might not cover the CashSmashers in the case of severe negligence. Then again, the contestants hadn't heard from the boys since the stunted, slightly nervous voiceover. Maybe they *were* panicking, buying time while they figured out how to cover their arses. He looked out the window at the drone. They were still here. Watching. That made it normal, right? *Normal?* He thought, Jesus, what even *was* normal anymore?

Besides, if violence generated views . . . money is a classic motive for murder.

His unease wouldn't leave him. He'd heard whispering in the corridor when he'd woken, alongside that strange scraping sound. May said she hadn't heard it. Michelle had told him it was Lisa and Adam and that there'd been yelling, before, from one of the bedrooms. Lisa had slept, or not slept, down that end of the house. She'd clearly had a conversation, heated or otherwise, with Adam. Or perhaps she'd heard something. Ryan thought of how Ned had stormed out of the house. Something strange had happened down in the bedrooms. Was that what was being yelled about? Or was Michelle merely deflecting? Either way, Lisa had made it through two nights without the aid of duct tape or meditation, so she clearly had a strategy. He should try to interrupt it if he wanted to win this thing. His thoughts quickly corrected themselves:

he wanted to win *and* he wanted to make sure Adam was actually safe . . .

While he was thinking this, he'd idly drawn a fat kitchen knife from the block on the counter and tapped it against the marble. It was heavy, sharp. These were real knives, not props.

He slid the knife back into the block, as another unanswered question arose. If everything in here was supposed to be fake, why was one of the real knives missing?

TWENTY

Back in the corridor, heading towards the bedrooms to talk to Lisa about whether she too had heard Michelle and Adam's conversation, Ryan almost ran the wrong hand over his brow, but caught himself just in time. At first he'd not taken seriously how hard this competition could really be. But now the psychological torture was setting in. As he was sleep-deprived and hungry, it took a lot more of his focus to keep his hand on the wall. They'd stopped feeding them, he realised – maybe to hurry things up, or maybe they were just busy with . . . *something else*. Things didn't make sense anymore. His vision was a little bit fuzzy. There was a throbbing at the base of his neck. When he moved, it felt like his mind went first and his body followed, like he was pulling himself through honey. In truth, he just felt a little bit dimwitted. A little bit undercooked. Was that why he believed the body in the pit was real? Or was that why he believed it wasn't? He didn't know what he believed.

He saw the droplets of red, spaced out every few centimetres on the carpet, as he walked along the corridor. As he got further from the main room, the droplets got smaller in size. If Adam had been stabbed in the bedroom, he would have been going the opposite way

Ryan was going now, so the amount of blood was steadily increasing with Adam's imagined footsteps. Ryan had no idea how people bled when they got stabbed. Did that fit, to grow from a drop to a splash? Or did what he was seeing better fit a teenager with a bucket, flicking a splosh of red paint every couple of steps?

He felt foolish for even considering the possibility; it was surely what the CashSmashers wanted. But if it was real, and *none* of them moved . . . He thought back to the first night. There had been six of them playing and only *one* responded to the actress's screams. One in six. Ryan felt ashamed. He'd tried to peel the tape off, but had he really tried hard enough? He'd thought it was real at the time. He'd still made a conscious choice. One-in-six odds on human compassion. You wouldn't even bet on that.

Lisa was in the ensuite, door closed, when Ryan came into the bedroom. His knock was answered by a groggy reply of *just a second*, and then Lisa emerged, rubbing her eyes with one hand. They negotiated their arms over and under each other, Lisa exaggerating the difficulty by getting tangled in his elbow.

Ryan didn't need to use the bathroom, but he stood in front of the bowl for thirty seconds, flushed anyway and washed his free hand with liquid soap. There was a rolled-up towel on the floor. A small camera, a GoPro, was fastened at chest height on the opposite wall to the toilet, no cords snaking from it. Unlike the cameras in the rest of the house, peering down from the roof, this had a horizontal line of sight. The single taped line on the wall was still there, to keep the contestants' hands in view of the camera without compromising their privacy, though Ryan still doubted it was legal to film inside a bathroom. He was half expecting the strips of tape to have been removed – he'd suspected maybe that was how Lisa had been sleeping – but it was untouched.

When he came out, Lisa was sitting on the bed, back propped up by pillows, one hand stretched out to the wall beside her. The covers were an awful vomit of flowers, with a lacy trim, the type found exclusively at grandparents' houses. The window behind her held a flowerbox stacked with succulents. The sun was on the other side of the house, so the room was slightly dim.

'You seem pretty comfortable down here,' Ryan said, lingering at the foot of the bed.

'I'd rather compete with myself than other people.' Lisa shrugged. 'Sounds like all kinds of crazy stuff is going on out there.'

'That's one way of putting it.'

Lisa's eyes lit up. 'You *believe* it, don't you?' Then she looked at his hand, still on the wall. 'Not enough, though, obviously.'

'I just feel like . . . I don't know. You know those horror movies where everyone makes all the wrong decisions? It feels like we're kind of there. The bit where everyone's on the secluded island and the storm's coming and the last boat is leaving and the audience, because, well, I guess we do actually have one of those'—he waved his free arm at the cameras in the roof—'is yelling at us to get on the damn boat.'

'Be my guest.' She pointed to the door.

'And that's exactly the problem, isn't it?'

There was a bang on the window, hard enough to rattle the frame. Ryan flinched, grabbed his elbow and steadied his arm. Lisa hadn't even blinked.

'Those idiots have been doing that all night.' She rolled her eyes. 'Trying to make us jump, eliminate ourselves.'

Ryan thought of the slamming door, Adam's nervous eyes, jerked from sleep, his hand on his wrist, steadying his shaking hand, which must have been only a sliver of skin away from leaving the wall. There was another question, adding to his doubts: if Adam *was* a plant, if he was only there to, for want of a better word, 'die' midway through, he'd seemed awfully desperate to stay in the game.

Ryan peered out the window but couldn't see anything. 'Is that what happened to Ned?'

Lisa looked like she was about to burst out laughing.

Eventually he'd find out, when he got home and watched the uploaded video, he supposed, depending on how it was edited. Ned's outburst rang in his memory: *if you even think about . . . footage . . . fucking kill you.* 'You think it's funny?'

'To get eliminated while taking a shit?' she snorted. 'Yeah, I think it's pretty funny. He was extra mad because it was my fault. He jumped out of his skin when I went in there *accidentally*.' She winked.

Well, Ryan thought, that explained why he didn't want the footage used. Ryan imagined Lisa bursting in, knowing full well Ned was using the toilet, his frantic reaction to cover himself, using both hands. It was ingenious. Maybe that was why she'd been camping out down here, waiting for people to use the ensuite. It also explained why Ned was furious, not only at being first out, but at the fact he'd been eliminated on the toilet. Being a laughing-stock was one thing, being a laughing-stock *on the internet* was on a whole different scale. That humiliation would follow him around forever.

Of course, everyone had their own strategies. The surfer's had been to be antagonistic, May's was mind games, Michelle's was meditation and Lisa's – well, it was the simplest and yet possibly the cleverest of them all.

'Did Adam come down here last night?'

'To use the bathroom? Sure.' She was suddenly defensive. 'But it's not like we set up a tent with cosy blankets and told ghost stories and talked about boys. People come and use the bathroom.'

'Did he have a knife with him?'

She thought about that, then shook her head. 'No. He didn't have one *with* him when he got here. And he didn't have one *in* him when he left, either, if that's what you're wondering.'

Ryan decided to change topic. 'How have you been sleeping?' She looked well rested, which meant she had come up with something to lower the risk of using the bed.

'I'm still playing.' Her smile turned suspicious. 'I can't tell you all my secrets.'

'Maybe just one more question. I just need some help piecing together what happened last night. Adam comes in to use the bathroom and you try to embarrass him like you did Ned, but he doesn't fall for it. That's why the two of you were arguing. Am I close?'

'What?' She looked both exposed and confused. 'That argument wasn't me and Adam. That was him and the other lady, out in the corridor. You know, the uptight one. Not your pal.'

'My pal?'

'You know, the one you've been getting cuddly with? She's working you over, by the way.' She whistled, holding up a pinkie finger, as if to imply May had Ryan wrapped around it. 'Anyway, not her – the older one.'

Ryan already knew it couldn't have been May, given that they had both been taped to the wall. 'Adam was arguing with Michelle?' he clarified.

'Yep. Out in the corridor.'

'About what?'

'What do you think? Michelle's a stickler for the rules. I heard words like *unfair*, you know, *cheating*, the same kind of stuff she threw at you when you got out your tape on the first night. I assume he took his hand off the wall, or she thought he had, and she was laying into him about it. I heard that. Anyway, no air horn, soooo . . .' She dragged it out as if the answer was obvious.

'She told me he bumped into her, almost knocked her off the wall,' Ryan said. 'She thought it was unfair. But she said she heard the two of *you* arguing.'

'Adam and I . . . Look, we had a . . . let's called it an animated conversation. But Michelle and him, that was a proper argument,' Lisa insisted.

'How mad was she? Like, was she aggressive?'

'Was the argumentative middle-aged lady aggressive?' Lisa almost couldn't get the sarcasm out through her laughter. 'I mean, sure. But you don't really think . . . well, *that* . . . do you?'

'Michelle said that it was you and Adam who were doing the yelling. What was your *animated* conversation about?'

'Yelling? No way. I don't know what's she's talking about,' Lisa said – too quickly, Ryan thought. 'Are you accusing me of something you don't even know is real?'

'I'm just trying to think it through,' he said. 'The blood starts at the door to this room.'

Lisa was being so casual it was difficult for him to think straight. But he could see why: down the other end of the house, behind a closed door, the body in the pit seemed miles away. The fear, the glint of the knife, the sight of the blood, that strange metal-air taste, had all faded already into a sort of surreal otherness. The rest of the house was the warped funhouse. In here, talking to her, the idea that it was just a game became easier to believe by the minute.

'Well, I don't know what to tell you. Adam wasn't bleeding when he left and no one else who came in to use the toilet was bleeding either.' Lisa sighed in a way that was almost pitying. 'I know these guys, I watch their stuff. It's a mind game. They're screwing with us and you're buying it. They're young and they're out of the box sometimes, but they're not psychopaths. They would have called the police if it were real. Trust me.'

'What were you arguing with Adam about, then?'

'So you don't trust me that much,' she said with a chuckle. A familiar phrase flickered through his mind: *literal psychopaths.* 'It's none of your business. But I didn't hurt him.'

Another crash against the window interrupted them and, this time, whatever had been thrown had left a thin, hairline crack in the glass. Lisa snapped, hauling herself off the bed and yelling through the window. 'Get out of here! How about instead of throwing rocks you find us some damn food? Do you plan on feeding us today?' She turned back to Ryan. 'See, this is all part of it. They want us on edge, so they've stopped feeding us, in case you haven't noticed. And these bumps in the night, slamming doors or throwing rocks at windows, are just to jangle our nerves even more. I can see them scurrying around the garden sometimes. Eurgh. *Boys.*' She took a deep breath. 'You think they'd really be bothering us like this if they had a *real* murder to worry about? It's not worth it.'

Ryan made to leave. 'Thanks for the info about Adam. It's helped put my mind at ease.'

'Has it?' She seemed surprised, sort of pleased with herself. 'Listen: real, fake, it doesn't bother me. There's four of us left. I'm here to win. You know what? Part of me hopes there *is* a killer. If they pick a couple more of you off, they'd probably be doing me a favour.'

TWENTY-ONE

When Ryan re-entered the corridor, the basement door was ajar, revealing a carpeted staircase. It turned at a right angle at the bottom, where a soft grey light illuminated the last steps.

Luckily the staircase formed a corridor and didn't just have a banister, so Ryan could walk down it and keep his hand in contact with the wall. Except the turn at the bottom was to the opposite side. It was like some stupid puzzle. He leaned in, pulled the door shut, walked across it, hand touching the door, and reopened it. Now he was on the correct side. He looked down the stairs, weighing it up. He looked back into the house. There was no noise from either end. Everyone was in their endgame now; they'd chosen their last stand. Without the tape, Ryan didn't have another night in him, he knew that. And he'd found his last advantage behind a closed door. It was worth a shot, wasn't it?

'Hey.' He waved at the corridor camera. 'Am I allowed down here?'

He wasn't sure what he expected. A voice through the speaker? An air horn? But he got nothing, just the silent house, as he talked into the empty lens, the overbearing black glass eye. He was losing, as Lisa would have put it, the battle with himself.

'Okay, then,' he said, placing one foot on the top step. It was a rash decision, he knew, but he was restless, irrational and ready to take some risks. Also the damn living room was giving him the creeps. He didn't want to go back there and have to think about Adam's maybe-fake, maybe-real body. One of the CashSmashers must have unlocked the door anyway, he figured. They *wanted* him to go down to the basement. He looked back up at the camera. 'But if you blow that horn, I'm taking the bag of money.'

He pulled his hand around the corner.

Nothing happened.

All right, then, he thought, quickening his steps down the rest of the stairs. They levelled out three steps around the turn. There was a short corridor, which he figured ran parallel to the corridor above him, a small bathroom on the left and a laundry room on the right, and then it opened up into a huge rumpus room. It was circular, like the main room above, except instead of glass, the walls were literally the craggy rock of the cliff. There was a gigantic wall-mounted television on his right, a pool table on his left and a glass-doored wine cellar in the back corner with an LED-lit door. Directly across from him was a window and a second door. The window was partially covered in vines but looked out onto the ocean. This must be the cliff-side garden area and the stairs that led up to the pool gate, which he'd seen from the lookout when they'd first arrived. He dragged his hand around the cave, the only word he could think to describe it. It was awesome. If he hadn't wanted to win before, he did now.

But what caught his attention wasn't any of the luxurious fittings.

It was the source of the soft, grey glow.

The giant television was on, the light coming from a black and white image playing on the screen. It took Ryan a moment to realise what he was looking at, but now he saw it was the outside of the house. The image was panning back and forth along the cliff-side windows, zooming in and out. It was the footage from the drone.

Ryan felt doubt creep in again: there was no denying the door had been deliberately unlocked, and that this footage was playing so that whoever came down here would see it. He remembered how the digital safe had clicked open, as if on cue, as he'd opened the cupboard door in the bedroom. It was hard to believe this hadn't been done for *him*.

From the outside, the drone camera caught a wide-angle shot of the main room, showing most of the pit, with glimpses of the corridor and the kitchen. Ryan looked into the pit, where Adam had been lying when he'd left the room.

The pit was empty.

His relief that it *was* a game after all was short-lived, cut off when he noticed that the footage was black and white because it was night-vision, the fireplace showing as an over-exposed flare of brightness. He could see the grey shapes of people scattered around the room: Michelle in her spot against the feature wall and him and May taped to the wall, next to the table. Adam was nowhere to be seen. Lisa, he knew, was down the other end of the house. This wasn't a live camera. It was recorded video from last night.

The timer in the kitchen – now a luminous grey on screen – ticked upwards. Ryan watched the screen, waiting for movement. If someone had put this video up for him, what did they want him to see?

Suddenly someone on screen started to move.

At the same time, Ryan heard a voice from the stairs. In the dim light from above, May's figure was a dark silhouette. She whispered slowly, each word laden with regret.

'Please don't watch that, Ryan.'

TWENTY-TWO

Dark thoughts ran through Ryan's mind. Memories of everyone telling him that May was playing him. Lisa holding up her little finger. Ned's mocking imitation of her voice. Michelle's insults. And now May was a dark shadow in the hall, telling him not to watch the footage from last night, scared of what he might see.

He would have felt more threatened, but May still had her hand on the wall. That relaxed him. She was still playing. How bad could her secret be if she was still following the rules? If she wanted to attack him, she'd have to comically work her way around the circle or risk being eliminated. He was a safe distance from her.

'Is there something I should know before I watch this?' Ryan said, pointing to the screen where he'd just seen May lift her head, waking up.

But May couldn't find the words. She shook her head, resigned. 'Just . . . just . . . know that I'm sorry, okay?'

Ryan turned back to the television, his mouth dry. He wasn't scared of May, on the opposite side of the room, but he *was* scared he was about to witness a murder. No one on screen moved for a minute or two.

And then May, carefully, unpeeled her tape from the wall.

It hit him in the chest like he'd been punched. Something was deeply wrong in the house. Everything felt more real now. Sweat broke out on his brow, ice cold. While he'd been sniffing around what had happened last night, he hadn't suspected May, because he'd thought they'd both been stuck to the wall. Now he'd just watched May dissolve her alibi in one sweep.

What she did next on screen was another surprise. She *didn't* go to the kitchen and retrieve a knife. She *didn't* head down the corridor, knife swinging by her side, after Adam. What she *did* do was lean over . . . Ryan.

He closed his eyes, drew a deep breath and tried to steady his anger. He almost saw it before it happened, as it played out on screen. May was not only leaning over him, she was gently lifting his hand. Ryan remembered dreaming of his wife's hand, touching his. The idea that May had invaded his dream hurt more than what he'd seen her do. Then she stood up and disappeared down the corridor. She was back quickly, gone just long enough to reach the end and complete the loop so she was on the other side of the hallway, enabling her to come out into the kitchen. She crossed it and stopped near the bloody handprint on the window. Now across the pit from Ryan, she stood for a moment, fiddling with a small object, turning it over in her hand. Then she lobbed the thing into the fireplace. It landed in the fire with a bright white flash on the camera.

Ryan felt stupid. Betrayed. May had taken him in with her charm and warmth; they'd formed an unofficial team, kept each other's spirits up. They'd been friends. Or so he'd thought. She'd talked him into staying at first, when he'd wanted to leave, and he'd thought she was being supportive. But now he knew that she was worried about the night-time and wanted the money to still be in play in case she felt she was about to lose. Then, when it was down to five of them, she'd changed her tune, basically telling him to take the money (*That bag's looking pretty good now, isn't it?* she'd said), seeing the end in sight and wanting to be rid of him.

When that hadn't worked she'd stolen Ryan's tape, slid it off his wrist while he was sleeping. That much was not such a surprise; he knew someone had, even though he was disappointed it was her. The thing that surprised him was that she'd thrown it into the fire.

She'd been playing hard all along. The surfer had seen through her – sniping at her faked confusion upon waking to the woman's midnight screams. No one wakes up that slowly. May knew someone was screaming, she just didn't care. But she didn't want to look heartless to Ryan in case he stopped sharing his advantage. All she cared about was winning. But enough to kill Adam? It was only for a moment, but she and Adam had both been out of sight down the end of the corridor at the same time. Adam's arm *had* been stretched out towards the bag of money, Ryan remembered. He knew how important it was for May to keep the money in play; her attempts to influence him were evidence enough of that. If she thought Adam was going for it, might she have, sleep-deprived and irrational as she was, made a terrible choice? As a motive, it made just enough sense. But not quite enough. If the murder had been committed in order to win the prize, surely the murderer couldn't be sure the competition would continue. And even if they had correctly predicted that the CashSmashers' bloodlust for views would outweigh their moral conscience and they would let them keep playing, it was still a murder committed on camera. There was no way they'd be able to claim the prize if everyone had seen what they'd done.

'Ryan, I'm—'

'I'm trying to watch this, please,' Ryan said, not turning away from the screen. In the video, May was sitting still, looking into the fire. It was hard to tell in the dark if the look on her face was regret. But she wasn't the first to stand up – it was Michelle who was the next to move. Getting up to use the bathroom, as she'd told

Ryan and Lisa had confirmed. She walked carefully, supporting her arm at the elbow with her spare hand, taking no chances on a small slip-up. May stood just as Michelle stepped over the sleeping Ryan. Michelle had disappeared up the corridor by the time May walked around the pit, this time going around the glass circumference, also stepping over Ryan, before sitting down next to him. His own image stirred a little, disturbed by all the movement. Was that when he'd awoken to hear whispering? May said she'd heard it too. He'd asked her if the argument had woken her or if she'd already been awake. That was why she'd deflected his question: she didn't want him to know that she'd been fully awake, because then he might have guessed at what she'd done. It made so much sense.

Video-May was now settling into her sleeping position, trying to salvage the tape she'd taken off before. It was hard to tell, but Ryan thought she gave him a forlorn look before she carefully smoothed her strips of tape back onto the wall, slumped, and stopped moving. He was so focused on her, he only caught a glimpse of the movement in the corridor over her shoulder. By the time he focused on it, the television blinked, and the movement was gone.

It looked like a glitch at first, but then Ryan realised that Michelle had teleported back to her position on the wall. The timer on the counter had gone backwards. The tape was still on his wrist. The video had reset. They were playing it on a loop.

'They want us to turn on each other,' May said. 'This is the psychological part of it. Why is this video playing, down here? Why is the door unlocked? This is for you. They want you to see this.'

'You're one to talk about *psychological*. The way you've tried to talk me into either taking or leaving the money depending on how it suited you at the time.' Ryan was seething. 'I knew you were playing me. I didn't think you'd fuck me over, though.'

'I'm sorry, okay? I had to. I'm like you. I *need* to be here. I saw that in you as soon as we started. And you mentioned your money troubles. Everyone else, they just *want* to be here. The electrician was just here to impress his mates. The surfer didn't care about money, he'd just use it to fund another couple of vagrant years around the world, I don't know.'

'He's the only one who tried to help that girl,' Ryan responded, trying to make May sound petty.

It worked. She backpedalled. 'Okay, that was undeserved. My point is he didn't *care* about the money. And Lisa? She's another influencer. She's just here for publicity. And Michelle, a lady so obsessed with competitions she'd enter if the prize was a raffle ticket?' May took a breath, steadying her rant. 'But you *need* to be here, don't you? And so do I. So I came in here ready to do anything, and, yes, that included earning your trust and using it for my own advantage. I didn't want the money walking out the door so early – it was *my* back-up. Then when I thought I could actually win this, I wanted you to reconsider. But you told me about your wife, your daughter, and I saw how much you needed this. I knew you'd never give up, and that made you my biggest threat. I'm a psychologist, I can read people. I wanted you to leave. That's why I kept mentioning the bag. Adam messed that up when he made you think it was fake. So I thought when you found out your one advantage was missing, you'd take the risk and leave with the money. That would have taken out my biggest threat, and, out of everyone left, I would have been the only one who *needed* to win, and so I would have. I'd do anything for my parents.'

Ryan softened slightly, remembering her tone as he'd told her about Rita the first night. She'd understood. It wasn't about winning the house for themselves, it was about what the house could do for them. But just as he was understanding this, anger overtook sympathy. She hadn't tried to take this house away from just him, she'd tried to take it from his *daughter*. That thought riled him up again.

'The only thing I *need* is for you to stop talking. I'm trying to see—'

'I don't want this to hurt our—'

'Our what?' He whirled around. 'Our *friendship*? I'll be damned. Turns out sleep deprivation does cause hallucinations.'

May didn't have anything to say to that. Ryan refocused on the TV, mostly to stop himself from apologising, which he felt the odd compulsion to do. He felt foolish for feeling angry, partly because if his sinking gut was right, he had bigger things to worry about upstairs, and partly because he couldn't really begrudge her for simply playing the game they'd been asked to play. But it still shook him. It still felt like a betrayal. A little voice in the back of his head wondered why that was. This was possibly the longest consecutive time he'd spent with a woman who wasn't his daughter in years. Was that why it stung so much? He shook it off. He couldn't believe he was thinking about *that* right now.

On screen, he watched as for the second time May stood up, wriggled the roll of tape from his wrist, disappeared out of sight and then came back and taped herself carefully to the wall next to him. It didn't hurt any less seeing it again.

Except this time he wasn't only watching her, he was watching over her shoulder. The angle of the drone camera captured a little bit of the corridor, just enough to see the movement he had only glimpsed before.

It was Adam lumbering up the hall. He was only in frame for a second before, right at the edge of the screen, he bumped into Michelle, giving her a firm knock while he tried to walk past her. They had an animated discussion but, crucially, neither touched the other again. Michelle's back was to the camera, blocking Adam's body, but they each had one hand on the wall and the other in the air as they flailed in argument. Ryan could see both of Michelle's hands the whole time. The conversation was heated, sure, with some aggressive finger pointing, but no violence. It was exactly how Michelle had described it. Ryan figured this must have been the tense whispering he had half-heard when his sleep was interrupted. Then Michelle disappeared up the corridor, out of frame, and Adam staggered forward.

The footage cut, the loop replaying again, everyone's positions reset like a new game of chess.

'Holy shit,' May said. 'This is . . . real?' She said it like it was dawning on her for the first time.

Ryan nodded. He'd seen it too, the dull sheen of the knife sticking out of Adam's abdomen after Michelle had walked past him. It was just a glimpse before the footage cut, but it was enough. Their argument forgotten, Ryan and May watched the scene replay a third time. Adam was a blur coming out of the corridor; it was impossible to see if he'd already been injured by the time he reached Michelle. Except . . .

'Michelle doesn't touch him.' May summed up Ryan's thoughts. 'I can see both her hands the whole time. One's on the wall and one's in the air.'

'Yes,' Ryan said. 'And you didn't see him when you went down the corridor?'

'I . . . er . . .' May stuttered as she realised what Ryan was asking her. Michelle, with both hands free, had clearly left Adam untouched. It was May and Lisa, sequestered in the bedroom away from the drone camera, who didn't have alibis. Them and the CashSmashers, Ryan reminded himself. They were keeping them playing, still watching, for a reason. Just like there was a reason they were playing this footage now. 'No. I didn't see him. Or Lisa. I didn't even go into the bedroom or the ensuite, I swear. I only used the corridor because it let me get to the firepit without stepping over you. Now that you mention it, I thought I heard a groan from the bedroom. Hang on . . . you're saying he was stabbed *before* he bumped into Michelle?'

Ryan's mind was racing with the same questions. Had Adam been stabbed *before*? Was that why he'd knocked Michelle: he'd been stumbling and injured from the bedroom? How had he made it all the way down the corridor, stopping for an argument along the way, with a knife in his gut? Had Michelle simply not noticed? Or maybe she had noticed, but he already knew she didn't believe anything in this house: it wasn't inconceivable that Michelle would have taken one look at the knife, scoffed and said *nice try*. Did Adam then, sleep-deprived and sense-starved, his injury ignored, decide to try to go for the money? Or had he panicked and thought taking his hand off the wall would cue the air horn, unmasking his attacker?

But the air horn hadn't gone. Why not? Ryan had three theories. First, the one he hoped for: that it wasn't real after all, and Adam was in on it. Second: Michelle had told him that the CashSmashers had made more money than it cost to settle the lawsuit from their negligence in a previous video. He remembered her asking him, *how much do you think they'll make if we start killing each other?* If views were that valuable, and no doubt everyone in the *world* would watch something like this, the guys might have seen it happen and decided to let it play out anyway. They might have even *wanted* it to happen. It seemed ridiculous, not to mention immoral, but it also felt like it might be true. The third – and scariest – theory was that maybe they didn't even know what had happened themselves. That would explain why they hadn't called the police, why they asked them to keep playing, if they were using the time to cover their defence. But one question lingered: how can you commit a murder unseen in a house full of cameras?

Were they not watching their every move after all? Ryan remembered what Lisa had told him about the teenagers: *slamming doors or throwing rocks at windows*. It all felt important, but he couldn't yet see the links between everything. Something circled his mind but refused to crystallise.

Above all, Ryan still couldn't convince himself that it was real enough to give up the game. Anything in this house could be a trick; that was the cleverness of the competition. The only thing he could be certain of was *his* hand on *this* wall. His mind was mush and so much of what had happened in the house hadn't been the way it looked. No. That wasn't true. He could convince himself it was real enough, but he didn't *want* to be convinced.

Ryan felt shame ripple through him. He'd promised himself he'd never let the wish for that ticket consume him again. And now here he was, cashing in everything for another ride. He'd gone back on everything he'd told Lydia that morning out the front of the supermarket. He imagined her sitting, knees up under her chin like she always sat at the computer, watching the CashSmashers' latest video, excitement quickly fading to confusion and then to pain as she watched her father unravel piece by piece, every bit of advice he'd given her revealed as a falsehood.

He looked at his hand. He knew now that he had to quit. The damage was done, and the only thing he could do now would be a small redemption, but he had to try. He'd quit and check on Adam and if it was all a trick, so be it. The CashSmashers could have the last laugh, but it wasn't worth the risk that it might be real. That he'd have to see the hurt on his daughter's face. The same look she'd given him at the start of all this would be the look that ended it. He went to take his hand off the . . .

Something cracked open in his mind. Something about that morning with Lydia.

The thought that had been circling in his brain, just out of reach, finally snagged. He managed to latch on to it and everything unspooled at once, clear as if he'd been awake when it happened. Because something *had* happened last night. And it had happened while he was asleep. And now he thought he knew what it was.

'What is it? What, Ryan?' May must have seen his expression change – the look of discovery dawning. 'Ryan, talk to me!'

But he ignored her. Instead, he was waving at the camera in the roof, talking to the ceiling.

'Hey! Hey! Get in here now.' Ryan hoped this room was mic-ed up. 'You'll want to listen to me. You've been keeping us playing because you don't know what happened. You think that if we have it out with each other you'll be famous. That's true, but how about I catch a killer for you? There's an episode worth watching. So get everyone in the main room, and for God's sake, call the police.'

'What the hell is going on?' May cried.

'Adam's really dead. And I know who killed him.' He lowered his voice and turned to May. 'Not only that, but I know how I'm going to win this damn house. It's time I learned to play dirty like the rest of you.'

TWENTY-THREE

'So . . .' May whispered as she followed Ryan up the corridor. 'Are we still playing? Should I take my hand off the wall? I will, you know. If you tell me to.' She said it like an apology.

Ryan had been dragging his fingertips along the wall too, as they went up the stairs and back into the main house. May, behind him, had kept her gaze locked on his hand. She *believed* he knew something about Adam's murder, but still the Pavlovian response, drilled into her from three days of trickery, from the lack of sleep, made her doubtful. She wouldn't go first. She refused to be made a fool of.

Ryan couldn't really blame her. And, thinking about how absurd it was that they were still playing, how compromised his own decision-making had become, he decided that her throwing his tape into the fire was, perhaps, not such a big deal after all.

'We're still playing,' Ryan said firmly. 'These idiot teenagers put all of us at risk. They've avoided responsibility for everything they've done in the past, when people have been injured in their games before. And now someone's dead, and they've probably been sitting and watching us, Daddy's lawyer over their shoulder, figuring out how to use it to make them more famous with minimal consequences. I'm sure some fancy lawyer could get them off with a couple of years – months even. So we're going to keep playing, because we're *taking* their millions from them.' Ryan tried to deliver his speech with as much confidence as he could muster. He believed what he was saying, but he had that same niggling doubt, that same beaten-down mind-set as before. He thought he had it figured out, but he couldn't trust his own thinking anymore. Was he about to do something awful?

They emerged into the living room, where Adam still lay motionless in the centre. His blood had seeped deeper into the plush white carpet, no longer a deep crimson but a faded pink. The bag of money was still there. As Ryan walked through to the kitchen, Lisa bustled out from the corridor and joined him. Brayden and Lucas cluttered behind her, having entered from the front door. Lucas looked stressed, but better rested than Brayden, who had large bags under both eyes. A man tailed them; he wore a long black trench coat and had a crew cut. Private security of some kind. The third CashSmasher, the one who usually held the camera, hadn't joined them. Ryan supposed he would be the one to call the police, but then he heard the familiar buzzing of the drone outside. They wanted to get all the angles on film. Not so much had changed, then.

Ryan took a breath, looked out to the ocean and ran through everything one more time in his head. He turned it over every way he could think of, and when he was sure it was the only way all the pieces fitted, he turned back to the room.

'You boys are going to jail – let's start with that,' he said to Brayden and Lucas.

'We didn't—' Lucas began, but Ryan talked over him.

'But you already knew that part. Who's this bloke with you? A lawyer, a fixer? Someone expensive, no doubt. I'm guessing from the haircut that you're formerly from some military or government agency, but there's less money in working for the government than cleaning up some rich kid's mess, right?' Ryan knew this because it was the same type of heavy that came to collect his debts. The older man didn't say anything, just shifted uncomfortably from foot to foot. Ryan focused on the two teenagers. 'Now, there's no denying you all saw the potential in what happened here as soon as it occurred. You paid out heavily in your last lawsuit, and yet the game still made you money. Not only that, but it cemented you as online celebrities. Because more violence means more drama means more views. So when this happened, another example of extreme negligence, you knew it might be a goldmine. But you can't all have agreed to just go along with a murder.' Ryan turned back to the ex-agency guy. 'That's where you come in, Mr Fixer: you're here because you're trying to figure out how to get them out of it. But that's only half your job; you're really here so the others don't call the police, so they feel safe.' He looked squarely at Brayden. 'You might have convinced the others that it was worth keeping the police away for long enough to finish your show, but the real reason was that *you* caused this. Didn't you, Brayden?'

Brayden, the ringleader, tightened his jaw.

Lucas turned on him. 'What the fuck?'

'You murdered someone, f-for . . . *views*?' stammered Lisa.

'That's ridiculous. How could you even come up with that idea?' Brayden insisted. 'Yes, this is . . . good stuff – we'd be idiots to stop recording. But we're trying to figure out what happened last night, too. That's why he's here.' He nodded towards their protection.

'You've got cameras, though. Didn't you see it happen?' May said, echoing one of Ryan's own thoughts down in the basement. He thought he'd actually figured that out too, but he was leaving it for later.

'This doesn't sound like it's part of a game,' Michelle said slowly. Of course. She still believed she was playing.

'They're negligent, but they didn't kill anyone,' Ryan continued. He walked around to where he'd left the knife in the block, pulled it out with his free hand and looked at it. He walked out of the kitchen with it, around the pit, to the furthermost point of the glass, a safe distance from everyone. He held the knife loosely, but it gave him comfort, just in case this went wrong. 'When you asked us over the intercom to keep playing, in an attempt to make us think it was another trick, it was clear that there was a scuffle over the microphone. So not all of you were happy with the decision. I figure you're dominant enough to get your way, Brayden; you seem to be the boss, above Lucas and the Drone Pilot anyway. And all three of you wouldn't have watched the cameras all night; you'd take it in turns, so there would have been just one of you. That means that only one person made the decision to not sound the air horn, and Brayden, you look like you haven't slept much. But that's all just supposition. The real reason I knew you wanted us to keep playing is because you'd planned this to happen. *You* put the knives on the kitchen bench. Deliberately. And I know it was you, because when Lucas dropped off the pizzas he clattered through the cutlery drawers looking for a knife. He didn't notice they were in a block on the bench. He didn't know the knives were there.'

'This is ridiculous,' Brayden protested. 'I didn't kill anyone!'

'Not directly. But you knew that the more violent and the more extreme you made this game, the more viral it would go. You wanted us to turn on each other. I'm not saying you wanted a murder, but you wanted *something* to happen. Why else would there be dangerous weapons in a psychological experiment where you knew your contestants would be subject to the stress of sleep deprivation?'

'You told me they had to keep playing so the killer couldn't get away before we could identify them!' Lucas shouted, shoving Brayden and simultaneously confirming all of Ryan's theories. First, that Brayden *had* hoped they might hurt each other, even if it was hard to believe he wanted them to actually kill each other, and second, that they hadn't caught the killer on camera.

'Oh my God,' May said. 'You even subconsciously planted the *idea*. That's what you said, over the speaker, when we were arguing over the tape. That was your voice for sure: *objects in the house can be used*. That's psychological influence 101. You bastard.'

Brayden ran a hand across his jaw. His cheeks were bright red, and he no longer looked like a millionaire celebrity; Ryan could now see the boy underneath all the excess. He looked like he was being lectured by his parents. 'I wanted it to be exciting, you know?' Brayden was pleading with his buddy now. 'I don't get it. He was fine when he . . .'

'Stop right there,' Ryan cut him off, not wanting Brayden's confession to spoil his plan.

The CashSmashers were culpable, but they hadn't actually wielded the knife. Someone else had done that. And Ryan needed to catch them out.

'You knew there was a limited time before we started getting suspicious,' Ryan continued. 'I mean, we're all in the headspace of the game, sure, but it's still a dead body on the ground. There's blood splashed through the corridor from the bedroom. You needed to speed it up. You stopped giving us food to get us to think less rationally. And when that didn't work, and you saw me asking questions, *doubting* your story, you showed me the tape of May last night. Everything in here is designed to influence us psychologically: the duct tape, the bedrooms, that video. You wanted us to turn on each other again, to get your ending before it all fell apart.'

'Enough with the moral high ground,' Brayden said. 'If you know who killed him, just tell us already. I want this over with.'

'Hey, this is *your* game, remember? This is what *you* wanted. I'm just playing it,' Ryan replied. He'd got what he wanted out of

Brayden, who'd confirmed enough for him to take the next step in his plan. 'But you're right. Let's cut to the chase. You've all got something against Adam, so we may as well do this properly. Let's go through all our suspects.'

'May.' Ryan turned to her first. She tried not to show it, but he could see she was offended not only that she was a suspect, but that he'd started with her. He let her stew for a moment, everyone's eyes on her, which wasn't really fair, but he needed some petty revenge. 'You were down the corridor at the same time as Adam, out of sight of the footage I've seen. He looks like he was going for the money, which I know you thought of as your back-up plan. If you crossed paths, I wonder if you realised he was going for the bag? That could be motive enough there.'

'I told you, I only used the corridor to swap walls.' Her voice shook. 'He was in the bedroom. I didn't even see him in the corridor.'

Ryan, satisfied with that answer, moved on. 'Lisa and Michelle, both of you argued with Adam last night: each of you told me about the other. Lisa, none of us saw you in the bedroom with Adam, and obviously whatever is on camera isn't enough to know for sure. But Michelle says she heard you arguing, and May, when pressed, mentioned she thought she heard a groan. And the blood trail, of course, goes all the way to the bedroom.'

Lisa was going pale, while Michelle was listening intently but didn't seem alarmed, possibly still convinced it was part of the game.

'And Michelle, Lisa told me you were accusing Adam of cheating, of bumping into you, and we all know how much you like to play by the rules.'

'He almost took me clean off the wall. I thought there'd be some kind of penalty,' Michelle said simply. 'But I'm not going to kill someone over it.'

'I've got a few issues here. One is that I've seen the footage of Michelle and Adam arguing in the corridor, but not Lisa and Adam in the bedroom. I can see Michelle's hands, but Lisa, I can't see yours. And I have to take May's word for it that she didn't cross paths with him down the end of the corridor, because I also haven't seen that.' Ryan shook his head. 'So the puzzle I'm trying to solve is how Adam had the energy, after being stabbed in the bedroom or the corridor, to argue with Michelle, without her noticing, and *then* lie down to die.'

'So . . .' Lisa said slowly. 'Who are you saying did this?'

'I said I was going through all the suspects. There's one missing,' Ryan said. 'They'll help us understand what happened.'

'You need Josh?' Brayden pointed outside at the drone, which was keeping a steady hover, like a military helicopter about to unleash fire.

Ryan noted the drone pilot's name: Josh. He shook his head. 'He's not important. I just need people with motives to kill Adam.'

'We're all here,' May said, head swivelling, counting the contestants. Four left.

'No, we're not. What's the surfer's name?' Ryan asked.

'Olly,' Lucas said, confused. 'Short for Oliver. But we sent him home after he was eliminated.'

'Olly!' Ryan yelled. 'Quit skulking around the garden and get in here, I've got some questions for you.'

TWENTY-FOUR

Oliver slinked in through the kitchen door. He'd been out by the pool, hidden from the convex windows but close enough to hear. He had the ability, having been eliminated, to raise both hands in the air as he entered, shaking his head vigorously.

'I didn't have anything to do with what you're talking about . . .' He looked into the pit at Adam's sprawled body. 'Oh, man. Shit. Is that . . .?' His eyes widened, realising why he'd been brought in. 'I thought this was just . . . I hadn't seen this . . . I couldn't go in front of the windows or you'd see me, I only just heard you talking about it. Really!' He ran over to Adam, sliding into a crouch next to the body. His hands hovered around the knife, as if wondering whether to pull it out, and then his fingertips went to the boy's throat, pressing. He checked him over, then looked up at the room accusingly. 'Why are you fuckers still playing?'

'The police are on their way,' Lucas said. Ryan was relieved to hear the ring of truth in his voice.

'This isn't fun anymore,' Lisa said.

'It's real,' Ryan said, giving up the masquerade. 'Somebody

stabbed Adam last night, in a house full of cameras, and almost got away with it.'

If there was a time to run, it would have been that moment. But no one moved. Hands stayed on the wall. Everyone still bluffing.

'Oliver,' Ryan said calmly, 'you were upset at Adam because you felt like he was the reason you were eliminated. He was the one with medical training, and he ignored the woman's screams and cries for help, so you were the one who had to go out and help her, which got you eliminated. You thought he was a coward and that your elimination was his fault. So after you were supposed to leave, you didn't – you stuck around, wanting revenge.'

'Revenge is a strong word for throwing rocks at windows and slamming doors.' He shrugged. When Lisa had told Ryan that someone had been throwing rocks at her window all night, he had thought it was strange for the CashSmashers to focus on harassing her when they had either a major psychological game to play with a fake murder or a real death to deal with. He'd been right: it had been Olly in the garden all night, annoyed at those who were still playing. 'I was trying to scare him off the wall, okay? Yeah, I was mad. But I didn't do this.'

'He wasn't inside the house,' said Lucas. 'We would have seen it on the cameras.'

'I know,' Ryan said. 'But Olly, you did see into the bedroom, didn't you? You mainly wanted to eliminate Adam – that's why you tried to scare him by slamming the kitchen door. Did you follow him down to the bedroom and try to rattle him there? Lisa complained you'd been throwing rocks at her all night. You knew Adam went *into* the bedroom, but until just now you didn't know what happened to him after he left it. You couldn't get a look into the main room without Michelle or me seeing you, as we were facing the pool, or setting off the sensor light during the night, and he's lying low in the pit, out of your view, so you assumed he was still in the bedroom. So my question for you is, did you see what I think you might have, in the bedroom last night? Did you hear what Lisa and Adam were yelling at each other about?'

Oliver swallowed. 'You mean . . . her?' He pointed at Lisa. She'd gone from pale to ashen. He sighed, his tone almost apologetic. 'I'm not sure I saw them *arguing* as such. She was . . . touching him.'

Both of the CashSmashers' jaws dropped. Lisa's forehead hit the wall with a *thunk*. Her lip was quivering in distress, listening to Ryan piece it all together. She could see now where he was going.

'Okay, let's tackle this,' Ryan continued. 'First of all, even the people with camera footage don't know who did the killing, which leads me to assume two things.' He turned to the CashSmashers. 'First of all, *Adam* must have been the one to take the knife from the knife block originally. Because if you'd seen the murderer take the knife, it would be cut and dried – we'd be done already. But we're not, which can only mean that you saw the *victim* take the knife. Secondly, because you didn't see the actual stabbing, I'm assuming there are gaps in your cameras' coverage. Am I right?'

'We're monitoring most of the house, but . . . we were relying on a bit of self-policing, yes,' Lucas answered.

Brayden said nothing, still sulking.

'Like the bathroom, for example.'

Lucas nodded.

'That's where Lisa's been sleeping,' Ryan said.

'Are you serious?' Michelle spat.

'The camera in there isn't even plugged in, and that model only has a few hours' battery life,' Ryan said. 'It's a prop to make us *think* we're being watched. The bathroom is a blind spot.' He turned to Lisa. 'You probably figured it out quite early, when you got Ned eliminated in there. Maybe because there was a delay in his elimination, you realised they weren't watching it. Or maybe you just pieced together the ramifications, legally and ethically, of filming the damn toilet. Either way, you've been staying down there since then, because you've been sleeping on the toilet floor. I saw the rolled-up towel you used as a pillow.'

'It's not what you . . .' She took a deep breath, tried to steady herself, but the tears started to flow anyway.

'Isn't it?' Ryan continued. 'Adam figured out you were sleeping in the bathroom. He confronted you in the middle of the night. But he didn't want you eliminated; he wanted something else. The CashSmashers didn't see it because they don't have a camera in there, but Olly saw it through the window. And May heard the groaning in the corridor.'

'He brought the knife because he thought it was funny,' Lisa sniffled, 'so that he could feel powerful, I guess, while he bragged about how he was going to tell everyone I'd been breaking the rules. I begged him. I said I'd do . . . anything.' Then she started yelling, a dam unleashed. 'He made me . . . touch him. Okay? Are you happy? If you need it in words. And then I yelled at him for what he *knew* he was doing. But I *didn't* kill him.'

'And he brought the knife for this little power game,' Ryan said. 'Maybe he put the knife down in the bathroom, and as he turned to leave you saw it and realised you were in a room with no cameras. You made your decision then. He stumbled out into the corridor, the blood spots increasing as he walked and bled more, with the largest patch of blood in the corridor where he staggered into you, Michelle. You were so pissed off you didn't notice he was hurt. We know you talked about someone cheating – May overheard that – but I think Adam was actually trying to tell you how Lisa had been sleeping. But you were too angry and you wouldn't listen. So he kept moving. And when he took his hand off the wall he realised no one was watching the cameras, and no help was coming. And here's what removes your motive, May: he wasn't going for the money.

He was going for the fire. He's a med student; he was going to try to cauterise the wound to stop the bleeding.'

Ryan paused for a moment, waiting for it all to sink in. Then everything started happening quickly, exactly as he'd planned it. The fixer produced a set of zip-ties from his pocket, the type police use instead of handcuffs, and began to advance on Lisa.

'No. It . . . it wasn't like that,' she stammered, edging away, her hand trailing on the wall, still refusing to quite believe what was happening and to let go. 'Everything up to the bit where I'm supposed to have hurt him, I'll admit. But I swear . . .'

The fixer finally spoke. 'Come on, sweetheart. My clients would like some time to get all our stories straight. It's best you come with me.'

She shook her head, a terrified little movement. Her eyes darted across to Ryan, blazing with anger. He avoided her gaze, unable to look at her. This was part of the plan, but not the part he'd been looking forward to. Then, snake-like, the fixer reached out, grabbed Lisa by the shoulder and spun her around. She was on her knees, then her front, and then he was hauling her up, half-carrying, half-dragging her to the entrance.

Both of her hands were laced behind her back, neither on the wall any longer.

3 CONTESTANTS
REMAINING

TWENTY-FIVE

Ryan heard sirens in the distance, the sound whipped over the cliffs by the wind. He couldn't tell how far away they were, but the volume was steadily increasing. Outside, the drone hovered over the ocean, still watching, still recording. Just as Ryan had expected.

'Are we still playing?' he asked.

'Are you fucking serious?' Oliver asked.

'What?' Michelle jumped in. 'So we just get nothing? No one else has taken their hand off the wall, notice?'

She was right. May was still leaning on the wall, not having moved throughout the confrontation, and Ryan and Michelle hadn't either.

'Well, we probably have a couple more minutes before the police shut us down,' Lucas said. 'We could honour it.'

'What?' Brayden said, whirling on his partner. 'We can't still give them this place. We'll need everything we have to dig out of this.'

'After what you've done?' Lucas replied. 'Josh was right, man. This is sick. These people deserve our money. All of it.'

'You're going to jail, you know that?' May said. But, despite her words, she still held on.

'Well?' Ryan asked, as he walked around the glass. 'Am I going to win this place or not?'

'We owe you what we promised you,' Lucas said. 'If you guys agree to keep playing.'

'You're in, aren't you, Michelle?' Ryan had reached where she was sitting and was standing over her.

'You haven't beaten me in two days. If you think a couple of minutes is going to change that, sure, I'll play,' she said.

'I'll . . .' May was trying to analyse Ryan, but she couldn't. She sighed. 'Okay. I'll play.'

'Perfect,' Ryan said.

Then he raised the knife. He wasn't holding it loosely anymore, he had a firm, stabbing grip. The sunlight glinted off the blade.

'Ryan, think about this . . .' May held her free hand out in a placating gesture, though she was all the way across the room. Michelle shrunk into her corner. Olly tensed his haunches, like a runner on a starting block ready to leap at him. Brayden and Lucas just chewed their lips, seemingly having no idea what to do. Here was their finale, but even they hadn't thought it would end like this.

'Think about this. *Please.*' Michelle was cowering below Ryan, frantically begging. 'You don't have to do this.'

Ryan's heart was thumping. His mind was a mess. What he was about to do was insane, deranged, but in his starving, sleep-deprived, addled brain, it made crystal-clear sense. This was how he would win. He just hoped it made sense later on, when his sanity returned. His hand was sweaty where he gripped the knife, clenching so hard his knuckles were white. He had a flash of his daughter watching him, which made him loosen his grip slightly, but then he reminded himself why he was here. He'd bought the ticket. He wanted to win. This was the only way he knew how.

Suddenly Olly's voice reached him. Calm and soothing, it came through the clamour of May's and Michelle's protests. He was still hunched like he was about to leap, but he also had one arm out. He was patting the air, in a gentle *put it down* motion. 'Come on, man, you don't want to do this,' he said softly. 'Look at yourself. What are you doing?'

Ryan smiled, took a deep breath and said, 'I'm winning this fucking house.'

Then he brought the knife down . . .

. . . stabbing Michelle clean through the hand and pinning her to the wall.

2 CONTESTANTS REMAINING

TWENTY-SIX

There was a second of doubt as the knife went in.

Had he got this wrong?

What had he done?

And then the second passed in silence. It was the silence that convinced him. Michelle still hadn't screamed.

He scurried back to a safe distance as she started to stand up. She did it slowly, rolling her stiff neck, removing her coat. As she stood, her *entire arm* separated from her body. It pulled away at the shoulder and was left dangling from the knife.

Now standing free of the wall, Michelle raised *two* hands in surrender.

'Very clever,' she said. 'How'd you figure it out?'

It had been remembering everything he'd told his daughter out the front of the supermarket, what felt like forever ago, that had made things click into place. More specifically, it was the vitriolic rant from the street performer with the fake arm.

'You're the most motivated here,' Ryan said. 'You've played before, and you weren't going to lose again if you could help it. It was obvious you had some inkling of what the competition would